Dr. Rehan

and miles to go before I sleep

DR. AFTAB AHMED

INDIA · SINGAPORE · MALAYSIA

DISCLAIMER

This book is a work of fiction. Names, characters, places, and incidents are either the products of the author's imagination or used fictitiously. Any resemblance to actual persons, living or deceased, businesses, events, or locales is entirely coincidental.

Books by the Same Author

Rehan

Love Is Like a Rainbow

Embracing Life

Sunshine and Dewdrops

I Shall Rise Again

DEDICATION

To the tireless hands and hearts of **healthcare professionals**—

the doctors, nurses, and unsung heroes behind the scenes—

and above all, to our **patients,**

whose resilience and trust light the path forward.

This book is for **you.**

I've witnessed that smile of gratitude,
It's all that matters in the spaces where we labor,
Where life teeters on the razor's edge,
And hope blooms with every heartbeat.

I've also seen faces etched with silent sorrow,
Of life slipping away despite a fierce fight,
We carry the weight of every loss we hold,
A silent ache that lingers in our souls.

Before I dwell on life's fragile thread,
A call from the ER would pierce the air—
A new life hangs in trembling balance,
And I'd rise to fight another battle.

For we are the guardians of hope,
The quiet heroes in white coats,

With hearts aflame, we wage unseen wars,

In life's unyielding theater, we rise…

and rise again.

– Dr. Aftab

ACKNOWLEDGEMENTS

First and foremost, I bow my head in gratitude to Almighty Allah, whose boundless grace and wisdom gave me the strength and inspiration to embark on this journey.

To my parents, my guiding stars—Dad and Mom—your unwavering love, sacrifices, and belief in me shaped the person I am today.

To my wife, Reshma, my anchor and confidante: your steadfast presence, patience, and unwavering support carried me through every challenge.

To my beloved children, Shiara, Yaseen, and Farhan—your laughter, curiosity, and boundless energy brighten my world and remind me daily of life's purpose.

My heartfelt thanks to my brother and his family, whose affection, encouragement, and shared joy in storytelling fueled my resolve.

To my dearest friends—Jagannath, Fatima, Bindu, and Salma—I am deeply grateful for the time and care you devoted to reviewing my work.

Your thoughtful insights and editorial guidance were invaluable, and I truly appreciate your generosity and support.

To my professional mentors and colleagues—the brilliant doctors, compassionate nurses, and visionary executives—thank you for sharing your wisdom, experiences, and lessons that shaped my worldview. This book is a tapestry woven from our collective journeys.

To my patients, the heartbeat of my universe: your resilience, trust, and stories have been my greatest teachers. This work is dedicated to you, with humility and gratitude.

Finally, to every soul who crossed my path, offering advice, critique, or silent encouragement—this book exists because of you. Thank you for being part of its journey.

PREFACE

This book is the highly anticipated sequel to my debut novel, **Rehan**, picking up precisely where it left off, to continue the gripping journey of its protagonists, Rehan and Shabnam. Their story—fraught with passion, trials, and resilience—unfolds anew in these pages, delving deeper into the emotional and narrative arcs that captivated readers in the first installment.

While the words here are mine, this creative endeavor owes its existence to the unwavering support of my cherished family, friends, and readers. Their encouragement was the cornerstone of this journey, transforming inspiration into ink.

To those who walked alongside Rehan and Shabnam in their first chapter: welcome back. To new readers: prepare to step into a world where love and destiny collide, and where every ending is merely a prelude.

This book includes a prologue chapter for readers who haven't read the first book, as well as a recap of the story for those familiar with the previous installment.

Prologue

1984–2004

This story begins in 1984, when I was ten years old. I belonged to a middle-class family. My father, Salman, a bank manager, worked tirelessly to provide us with quality education. My mother, Farida, was a master of all things—revered for her wisdom despite her modest education. My brother, Imran, was my opposite: disciplined, sincere, and perpetually responsible. But my closest confidante was Dadima (Grandma) Rahima, whose patient ear and sage advice guided me through every childhood dilemma.

Sunshine School, where Imran and I studied, was a semi-trust institution with exceptional teachers. I approached life with a nonchalant, lazy attitude—for me, school was merely a place to study casually and revel with friends like Arun, Ashok, and Mohan. The notion of striving for excellence felt alien... until Shabnam entered my world.

Shabnam, our class captain, initially dismissed me for my carefree demeanor. Yet beneath my indifference, she glimpsed untapped potential. What began as rivalry blossomed into an extraordinary friendship, propelling me to become a formidable academic contender. By tenth grade, Shabnam, Sunil (our chief competitor), and I were locked in a battle for the top rank. When I grabbed the first place, Sunil reeled in disbelief, while Shabnam celebrated my triumph. We left school with bittersweet farewells, the future a blank canvas.

Fate reunited us at medical college. Together, Shabnam and I navigated storms of exams, heartbreaks, and self-discovery. Just as I mustered the courage to confess my love, tragedy struck: Shabnam's mother passed away, and she vanished. Years later, she revealed that her elder sister Roshna who settled in the U.S. urged her to continue her medical studies abroad. Shabnam admitted she'd loved me since our schooldays, but at the crossroads, with me clearing my postgraduate entrance exam and her being derailed by grief—she chose to pursue her ambitions in America. I remained determined to become a physician.

After graduating, I joined Hope Ray Hospital. Shabnam, meanwhile, completed her Critical Care fellowship in the U.S. and sought a position at the same hospital, hoping to reunite. But fate intervened again: I was to get engaged to

Muskaan, my sister-in-law's younger sibling. At the engagement, however, I learned of Shabnam's silent struggles and unspoken love. Muskaan understood my feelings for Shabnam and selflessly called off the engagement, urging me to chase my heart. Defying destiny, I flew to the U.S., resolved to reclaim what I'd lost.

*****

Massachusetts General Hospital loomed before me like a monolith of modernity, its glass-and-steel facade gleaming coldly under the overcast Boston sky. The sprawling campus buzzed with a controlled chaos—doctors in white coats striding purposefully, gurneys rattling over polished floors, the faint beep of monitors seeping through automatic doors. The air smelled of antiseptic and dread. My shoes squeaked against the sterile linoleum as I approached the help desk, my pulse pounding in my ears. The clerk, her face a mask of bureaucratic detachment, barely glanced up as I stammered, "D-Dr. Shabnam. Critical Care. Is she… here today?"

Her fingers clacked over the keyboard; the sound as sharp as gunshots. Seconds stretched into eternity. Then, a sigh. "No one by that name is in our system." She shrugged, already turning to the next visitor.

The words hit like a punch in the gut. I gripped the edge of the counter, knuckles whitening, as if the world had tilted off its axis. No. This can't be. Crushed, I staggered outside, grappling with despair. The cold wind clawed at my coat, carrying the tang of diesel and decaying leaves. I wandered blindly, past ambulances idling like silent predators, their red lights bleeding into the gray haze. My mind raced—was her hiring too recent? A flicker of hope: maybe administrative delays, a paperwork oversight. Where are you, Shabnam? The question echoed in my head, merging with the distant wails of sirens and a dissonant chorus that grew louder, sharper, until it was all I could hear.

Too late, I turned. The screech of tires ripped through the air. A streak of white—blinding, unstoppable—hurtled toward me. My arm shot up on instinct, a fragile barricade against the inevitable. Impact. The world exploded in a chaos of light and sound as the speeding ambulance struck me. For a fractured second, reality splintered—then collapsed into silence. The darkness was absolute, a velvet void swallowing time and space.

Fragments of my life flashed:

Dadima's storytelling…

Father's treasured library card…

Cricket matches at Evergreen Ground…

Shabnam's fiery debates…

Shiva's embrace…

Gold medals gleaming in my palm…

Shabnam's final goodbye…

Is this the end?

A voice sliced through the void: "Rehan, fight—don't leave me!" My eyes fluttered open to a blur and searing lungs. Rhythmic compressions pounded my chest.

"Head injury and traumatic pneumothorax—intercostal tube now!" a voice ordered. "Prep for intubation! Page Neurosurgery! Clear the CT room!"

Chaos swirled, yet I clung to faith—in God, in the hands fighting to save me.

When my consciousness returned, the words that greeted me etched themselves into my soul:

"Rehan, welcome back to life!"

"Finally! I found you!"

"I'm glad you did."

"It's time you came back into my life."

"Yes! Rehan, I will—forever."

There stood Shabnam, her smile radiant, eyes glistening with tears.

Chapter 1

In every end is a new beginning,
As seasons change and rivers flow,
Our lives evolve, letting us grow.
In the vast expanse of the night,
Let your dreams take flight, shining bright.

In the wake of that fateful day, I waged a merciless battle against all odds to cling to life, each breath a ragged symphony of pain and defiance. The sterile walls of Massachusetts General Hospital became my reluctant sanctuary for two interminable weeks, their bright lights draining the color from my world as machines hissed and whirred like mechanical sentinels guarding the threshold between existence and oblivion. Shabnam anchored me to the living, her resolve as unyielding as the steel beams framing the city outside. She refused to let me succumb, her voice slicing through the morphine fog: "You don't get to quit now, Rehan. Not after everything."

Shabnam managed the crisis with poise, notifying Imran of my mishap and reassuring him that she had everything under control. It took Imran a week to reach the US, navigating through the visa procedures. The hospital stay afforded me considerable time to reflect on bygone events. My mind was awash with thoughts. Shabnam, with her characteristic candor, addressed all my concerns.

One midnight, as snow blurred the Boston skyline, I rasped a question, "Why did you really leave India?" She didn't flinch.

"Because loving you felt like holding a lit match," she said, adjusting my oxygen tube. "And I was terrified we'd both burn."

Her candor, sharp as a scalpel, laid bare every unspoken truth between us. Ours was a dance of survival, stitched together by scars and stubborn hope.

It was no easy feat to convince my parents. I informed them that I had a minor accident and assured them of my swift recovery. They expressed a desire to visit, but I persuaded them that Imran's company was sufficient. Shabnam secured a rental apartment for us, ensuring our comfort during the stay. Weeks later, Imran and I returned to India, while Shabnam remained to fulfill her notice period at the hospital. The goodbye was a blade to the chest. Shabnam stood at JFK; her fingers intertwined with mine until the last possible moment.

"Three months," she promised, her voice steady despite the tears shimmering in her lashes. "Just let me honor my contract. Then I'm yours."

Although I was discontent with the separation, I was confident that Shabnam would soon return for good.

My parents were overjoyed and relieved at my return. They greeted me with a feast that night, their relief palpable in the heaping plates of biryani and the way my mother's hands fluttered over my healed scars. I had yet to reveal Shabnam's existence to them, preferring to keep it a secret. I guarded it closely—Shabnam's name lingered on my tongue, a bittersweet surprise I vowed to unveil only when she stood beside me. The following week, I met with Mr. Anand Krishna, Hope Ray's stoic administrator, in his office overlooking the hospital gardens. I informed him of my impending return and mentioned that Shabnam would soon join us. Her position as head of the critical care unit awaited her.

One crisp autumn afternoon, Muskaan, my sister-in-law Suhana's spirited younger sister, arrived unannounced at our doorstep. Sunlight filtered through the curtains, casting a warm glow over the living room where we sat. Her presence stirred a bittersweet nostalgia, the memory of our parted ways on the day of my engagement lingering like an unspoken shadow. She settled into the armchair across from me, her emerald scarf draped casually over her shoulders, eyes sparkling with mischief.

"Hey Rehan, glad to see you're well," she began, her voice laced with playful familiarity. "Shall we prepare for the Nikah?" she teased, leaning forward with a grin that crinkled the corners of her eyes.

I chuckled, shaking my head. "Muskaan, will you ever change?"

"Never!" she declared, tossing her curls defiantly. "Rehan, don't you recall my words? If you failed to find Shabnam, you'd have to return to me." Her tone softened, a flicker of genuine curiosity beneath the jest.

"Yes, Muskaan, I remember," I replied, my grin widening as Shabnam's face flashed in my mind—her laughter echoing through the quiet spaces of my heart.

Muskaan gasped, clasping her hands dramatically. "My God! You found her. It's written all over your face!"

"Yes," I confessed, my voice steady yet tender. "I found her before I lost myself." The admission hung in the air, heavy with gratitude. Muskaan deserved this truth. Years ago, when I'd hesitantly broken our engagement, she'd listened without judgment, her eyes brimming with quiet empathy. "Go find her," she'd urged, squeezing my hand. "You'll regret it forever if you don't try."

Muskaan listened intently, her playful demeanor replaced by warmth. "I need to surprise my parents," I finished. "Will you keep this secret?"

"Of course," she vowed without hesitation, her smile softening. "But you owe me all the details later."

As she rose to leave, sunlight caught the mischief returning to her eyes. "And Rehan? Tell Shabnam I'll steal you back if she ever lets you go."

We both laughed, the weight of the past dissolving into the golden afternoon light.

*****

December 31st, 2005.

The final day of the year hung in the air like the scent of winter jasmine blooming along Hyderabad's bustling streets. Over two months had passed since my return to India. Shabnam and I maintained constant contact. We spoke every night, her voice threading through the static of long-distance calls, weaving plans for her arrival. "Soon," she'd say, and I'd clutch the word like a lifeline. My parents were content with my recovery and attitude, unaware of Shabnam's existence. They were astonished by my positive outlook despite not having found Shabnam. Their smiles softened with relief, each time they saw me stride out each morning in my white coat, unaware that my heart pulsed not just for medicine but for a woman whose absence carved a quiet ache in my chest. Shabnam: her name was a whispered promise I carried like a talisman.

That day, after concluding my duties at the hospital by 5 pm, I drove directly to Ashok's residence. He was my childhood friend. No matter one's age, the company of friends always brings a sense of youthfulness. Ashok and I shared many wonderful adventures during our school days. On one occasion, we boldly skipped classes to enjoy a cricket match at home. Ashok made a decision to join the South-Central Railways and was making great strides in his career. As I drove toward Ashok's home, the city's labyrinthine lanes unfurled before me, auto-rickshaws darting like fireflies, vendors hawking marigold garlands for New Year's festivities. The golden glow of dusk settled over the rooftops, painting the sky in hues of turmeric and saffron.

"Hey Rehan, how's it going? Back to saving lives?" he greeted me with a smile.

"You know me, Ashok, I can't sit still for long. What about you? Climbing the ranks to your next promotion?" I inquired.

"Doctor Saab, keep me in your prayers. With luck, I'll achieve it by next year," he replied, beaming.

The creaking of the veranda door interrupted us. Kavita, Ashok's sister, emerged, her silk dupatta fluttering like a crimson wing. Time had sharpened her wit but not dulled her warmth.

"Rehan! Still chasing ghosts?" she teased, though her eyes showed concern. Kavita had been Shabnam's confidante long before she became mine. She was instrumental in helping me recognize and embrace my love for Shabnam.

"Since when did you swap Bangalore's gardens for Hyderabad's chaos?" I asked, deflecting.

"Since my brother promised homemade biryani and your dramatic love story," she retorted, arching a brow. "Well? Did you find her?" and I knew she meant Shabnam.

"Yes, Kavita. She'll be joining us soon," I assured her.

"Rehan, that's fantastic news!" Arun's voice chimed in from behind. Arun, like Ashok, was a cherished friend. My passion for literature was kindled by my friendship with Arun. We spent days journeying to the City Library, eager to immerse ourselves in the world of books. Those days remain etched in my memory as truly unforgettable. Arun served in the Indian Naval Academy and he often visited Hyderabad towards the year's end.

"Hey Arun! It's a small world indeed! This feels like a mini school reunion," I exclaimed, delighted.

"Let's celebrate this evening for new beginnings," Ashok said, his voice filled with optimism.

It was a delightful and heartwarming experience to reconnect with my childhood friends on New Year's Eve. We dined at Paradise Hotel, indulging in their renowned Hyderabadi biryani, a favorite of ours. As we savored each bite, our conversation drifted to the past. "You were fabulous with the cricket bat, Rehan," Ashok remarked, dredging up memories of our cricketing days. "Raju Bhai used to say you'd bat for India someday." The mention of our old mentor stirred something in me, a twinge of the "what if" I'd buried long ago. But the moment passed as Arun launched into an impression of our stern math teacher, and we dissolved into laughter, the years melting away.

Afterwards, we headed to Evergreen Ground, the playground of our youth, where a New Year's celebration was in full swing, complete with a large crowd and vibrant music. I anticipated it might get late, so I informed my family that I would be at Evergreen Ground with my friends and might return home after midnight.

The ground was alive with a spirited crowd, and among them, I recognized a familiar face—Raju bhai, our senior friend and former cricket team captain. Raju Bhai greatly encouraged me and provided immense support for my pursuit of cricket during my school days. He saw potential in me to become a good cricketer. Standing before me now, I could see that time had left its mark; he had aged considerably. Approaching him, I inquired about his well-being.

"Ah, Rehan! You've grown up," he observed after a moment's pause.

"You haven't changed a bit," I fibbed, aiming to brighten his spirits. He seemed gratified by my compliment.

"Rehan, you abandoned cricket for another pursuit. Did you find success?" he asked. Back then, I was passionate about cricket. However, I faced a tough decision: to continue playing cricket or to pursue my dream. I chose the latter.

"He's a top physician now, Raju bhai," Ashok interjected.

"Remarkable… I thought we lost a talented cricketer, but you've become an esteemed doctor," Raju bhai remarked.

"It's all in Allah's hands," I replied, feeling grateful.

My phone started ringing—it was Muskaan. Her voice cracked under poorly concealed excitement.

"Yes, Muskaan? What's the matter?" I answered, puzzled by her call.

"Rehan, drop everything and hurry to your old house, across from Evergreen Ground."

"What's going on, Muskaan?" I asked, curiosity piqued.

"Just come quickly with your friends."

I rallied Ashok, Arun, and Kavita, and we dashed to the old, weathered structure that once was our home, a repository of cherished memories from my childhood, family, and friends. The old neem tree still stood sentinel in front of the house. There, I found my parents and Muskaan waiting.

"What brings you all here?" I asked, bewildered. It was all so unusual. It didn't make any sense.

"Rehan, it's time for you to make a decision," my father stated, casting a glance between me and Muskaan. His timing left me confused.

"But Dad…" I started, only to be interrupted by Muskaan's giggling proclamation,

"I warned you, Rehan, you can't escape me."

As I grappled with the events unfolding before me, the air hummed with the whisper of neem leaves, their earthy scent mingling with the faint perfume of jasmine blossoms. And then, like a melody breaking through silence, she appeared. Shabnam stepped from behind the neem tree, her silhouette framed by the fading light, a vision in a flowing crimson dress that danced with the breeze. I caught my breath; time seemed to still. Weeks of yearning collapsed into this single moment, every unspoken word swelling in my chest. Muskaan's mischievous plot was clear now, but all I could see was Shabnam, the curve of her smile, the spark in her eyes, the way her presence turned the ordinary world into something luminous.

Clearly, Muskaan had orchestrated this ruse, and Shabnam was in on it. I had planned to surprise my parents with Shabnam's introduction, but now the tables turned. Shabnam moved toward me, each step a promise. She threaded her fingers through mine, her touch steadying the storm in my chest.

"You once told me roots matter more than wings. Look we are back to our roots!"

Over three decades had passed since we left this place to chase our dreams. Was this the conclusion of our journey, or merely the beginning? We each ventured down our own paths in pursuit of our dreams, confronting numerous challenges and surmounting obstacles along the way. Now, we stood, reunited at the very place where our journeys began.

"Life indeed comes full circle. Welcome back, Shabnam," I said, embracing her affectionately.

Then, as if on cue, cheers erupted and fireworks painted the sky, heralding the arrival of the new year.

Together, we raised our voices in unison, exclaiming,

"Happy New Year!"

In that moment, beneath the ancient neem and the vast, forgiving sky, I understood: Life and love were not destinations but the path itself, not straight, but a spiral, overgrown and wild and ours. We leave, we grow, yet the threads of our beginnings never sever. Instead, they pull us back, richer and wiser, to the places and people who first taught us how to dream.

2

CHAPTER 2

Even the darkest night will end,
and the sun will rise.

–Les Misérables

The early morning call jolted me awake—another urgent case at the Emergency Room. As a consultant at Hope Ray Hospital, such calls had become routine. This time, a 16-year-old boy was battling severe sepsis. Amidst the background noise, I could discern the harsh tones of someone berating the staff. The increasing aggression of patient attendees was a troubling trend. Just when I ended the call, my phone rang again. It was the CEO of Hope Ray Hospital, informing me that the patient was the son of a local MLA and urging me to attend to him immediately. The influence of local MLAs was well-known; they often wielded their power through intimidation.

I made my way to the hospital, knowing I would likely miss Shabnam, who was on night duty. It was our first wedding anniversary, and I had planned a special evening for us. Hope Ray Hospital, one of the city's finest corporate hospitals, was renowned for its multispecialty care and state-of-the-art facilities. Although the services were costly, they provided an ideal environment for medical practice. My rapid ascent to a consultant position was a testament to the management's confidence in me, and I was eager to excel.

The bright lights of the emergency room hummed overhead, casting a sterile glow over the chaos. When I rushed through the sliding doors, my shoes squeaking against the polished floor, the scene was one of controlled panic. The casualty doctor, a young man with sweat beading on his forehead, stood like an island in a sea of urgency, surrounded by nurses rattling off vitals and anxious relatives clutching at sleeves. His eyes locked onto mine the moment I entered, a flicker of hope cutting through the tension. "Thank God you're here," he muttered, barely audible over the din, before steering me toward the patient.

Harsha lay on the gurney, his slight frame dwarfed by machines and tubes. At first glance, he seemed younger than his 16 years, his cheeks flushed a dangerous crimson, chest heaving in a futile battle for air. The monitors screamed his distress: oxygen saturation plummeting to 82%, heart rate a frantic 140 beats per minute. A thin layer of sweat coated his skin, and his fingers had taken on a bluish hue, a haunting sign of respiratory failure. I pressed my stethoscope to his chest, hearing the ominous crackles of fluid-filled lungs. "Pneumonia?" I asked, though it was hardly a question. The junior doctor nodded grimly. "Worsening over three days. They tried home remedies first." My jaw tightened. By the time desperate families reached us, it was often a race against irreversible damage.

A man stepped forward, his tailored silk kurta at odds with the crumpled scrubs around him. MLA Manjunath's voice carried the weight of a man accustomed to obedience. "Dr. Rehan," he began, as though we'd met a thousand times, "I am Manjunath, the MLA of this province. Harsha is my only son. I want you to take good care of him. I have already spoken to your CEO." His gaze drilled into me, a silent challenge. I noticed the way nurses stiffened, how the resident doctor suddenly found the floor fascinating. Power, I'd learned, cast long shadows in hospitals.

"Every life here is important, sir," I replied, keeping my tone steady as the ECG blips. "Your son will get the same care I'd give my own."

His wife, a sari-clad woman clutching prayer beads, touched his arm. "Let the doctors do their work, Manju," she whispered, though her red eyes mirrored his fear.

" Of course, do your job, Doctor. But I expect only positive results," he said assertively.

It made me wonder: could doctors truly alter every outcome? If so, perhaps no one would die in this world. I was unsure why there was such skepticism surrounding medical care, or why people believe that applying pressure on doctors or healthcare providers would result in better treatment. As doctors, we treat every patient with the same level of commitment, and effort. If anything, pressure tactics could only serve to undermine the relationships between doctors, patients, and their attendants.

After the initial treatment and stabilization, we moved Harsha to the ICU. I sorely missed Shabnam's presence. She excelled at managing critical cases, but she had left the hospital after her night duty. Dr. Rajesh, her junior, was now on the morning shift. Rajesh possessed sound clinical skills and knowledge, and I trusted him.

"Blood pressure's soft," Rajesh noted, frowning at the readings.

I nodded, masking my unease. "Start norepinephrine. And get a blood gas analysis. I want to know his pH before we drown in acidosis."

The team sprang into motion, a well-practiced ballet of needles and lines. Outside the glass doors, the MLA paced like a caged tiger, his phone flashing endlessly. I understood his fear—the helpless rage of a man who could command roads built but couldn't will his son's lungs to clear. Yet with every order I gave, I felt the invisible weight of his expectations, the unspoken 'Your career breathes with my boy's'.

In the afternoon, during my second visit to the ICU, I noticed that Harsha's condition was deteriorating. His pulse raced, blood pressure dropped, and despite oxygen support, he remained breathless. The inflammatory storm was wreaking havoc.

"Dr. Rajesh, what do you think?" I asked the critical care specialist.

"Dr. Rehan, the patient is receiving the best and maximum treatment. If he gives us some time, we may be able to pull him through. Time is crucial," Rajesh replied.

"Yes, I understand. Harsha is on potent antibiotics, but his overwhelming inflammatory response concerns me. I fear time may not be on our side," I admitted.

"I believe we should discuss his prognosis with the parents. Additionally, the CEO wants an update on his condition."

"Agreed. I'll speak to them," I said, my apprehension growing.

It was a case fraught with challenges and high stakes. A young patient was battling severe sepsis, and we were determined to exhaust every possible avenue to improve his condition. As I contemplated additional measures beyond our standard treatment protocol, my mobile began to vibrate. It was Shabnam calling. It was around 4 pm. I was about to answer when I saw Harsha's father entering the ICU.

"Dr. Rehan, how is he doing?" he asked sternly.

"Mr. Manjunath, his condition is unstable. But we are doing everything we can," I replied.

"What do you mean by unstable?"

"He might require assisted ventilation."

"Dr. Rehan, I don't care how you do it, but I want my child alive," he asserted firmly and left the ICU.

I sat down with Dr. Rajesh to discuss further treatment options. There was one untried option: *Xigris*. This newly introduced product controlled the marked inflammation associated with severe infections. However, it was expensive, and uncertainty surrounded its utility.

"Dr. Rajesh, I think we should consider using *Xigris* in this patient." I presented my option to him.

"We haven't tried it before on anyone, and it's exorbitantly priced," Rajesh cautioned.

"Cost is not a factor here, and Harsha meets the eligibility criteria for *Xigris*."

"Be aware of the bleeding risks. We'll need meticulous monitoring."

"We can handle that," I decided firmly.

I instructed the pharmacy to provide the medicine immediately. By 6 pm, we had initiated Harsha on the new therapy. I glanced at my phone—six missed calls from Shabnam. It was late, and if I didn't leave now, my evening plans would be ruined. But I had to make a call first.

I dialed the CEO to update him on Harsha's condition and our treatment plan.

"Dr. Rehan, I hope you know what you're doing. We cannot afford to lose this boy," he said solemnly.

"I am doing my best, sir. I'll brief Dr. Rajesh and closely monitor the patient's progress," I assured him.

"Rehan, I cannot rely on anyone else. You must stay back until the patient stabilizes," he insisted firmly.

"But I have to…" I began, interrupted by the CEO.

"It's a VIP case. We can't take any chances. Please stay back," he concluded.

My plans for a beautiful evening were dashed. I needed to call Shabnam and explain. She hadn't answered my previous calls: she must be upset. Guilt and helplessness washed over me.

As the shift change approached, Dr. Rajesh approached me with a sense of relief.

"Dr. Rehan, it's good that you're staying back. The ICU doctor tonight is new and not very experienced."

"Who said the ICU doctor is inexperienced?" The voice sliced through the ICU's mechanical symphony—lilting, familiar, a melody that always found its way through chaos. I turned, and there she was: Shabnam, framed in the doorway like a painting I'd stared at for years but never truly seen. The harsh fluorescent light softened around her, as if even the hospital knew to bend for her grace. Her scrubs were wrinkled from the night shift, her hair hastily tied back, but her smile, that smile, was a sunrise after a decade of nights.

"Dr. Rehan," she said smiling, "you have the pleasure of my company, the ICU in charge herself!"

"But how did you know?" I asked pleasantly surprised.

"When you didn't answer my calls, I sensed something was amiss. After speaking with Dr. Rajesh, I swapped shifts to return for the night," she explained.

"Fantastic! I was worried you'd be upset," I admitted, my smile mirroring hers.

"Rehan, we both understand what truly matters. You taught me this: when the storm comes, you don't let your partner face it alone."

Her admission unraveled me. Shabnam had worked 14 hours already. She'd canceled the dinner reservations, the candlelit table, and a wonderful evening. All for this—for me, for a boy she'd never met, for the crushing weight of duty we both carried.

"Happy first anniversary, Shabnam!"

"Happy anniversary, Rehan!"

Perhaps it was the most extraordinary first wedding anniversary anyone could have—spent in a hospital ICU, surrounded by the stark realities of life and death. It didn't matter that we couldn't celebrate with our families; what mattered was that we were together, doing what we do best: saving lives. Thus, we commemorated our first year of marriage in the critical care unit, united in our commitment to a life hanging in the balance.

By dawn, Harsha's condition had markedly improved. It appeared that the infection and inflammation were getting under control, and he was on the path to recovery. His father, Mr. Manjunath, arrived as sunlight slanted through the blinds, his eyes heavy with sleeplessness. Just the previous day, he'd stormed through these corridors like a monsoon, barking orders at staff, his political authority clashing with medical protocols. Now, he hesitated at the threshold, his bear-like frame diminished by vulnerability. When I nodded toward Harsha's stabilized vitals on the screen, his shoulders sagged, not with defeat, but with the weight of fear finally lifted.

"Mr. Manjunath, your son is on the mend. He should be ready to leave the ICU within the next 36 hours."

"Dr. Rehan," he began, voice frayed at the edges, "when I saw him struggling to breathe yesterday…" He trailed off, fingers brushing against his son's face, a gesture startlingly tender. "I've faced election riots, public scandals—nothing compared to this helplessness."

Shabnam came forward and looking at Harsha said,

"Children have their own kind of resilience. They fight in ways we can't always see."

Mr. Manjunath turned to me; the politician's steel replaced by a father's raw gratitude.

"Dr. Rehan, thank you! The pressure on you was immense. Your composure is remarkable."

I was surprised by the swiftness with which his previously aggressive and tough demeanor softened into a gentle look and a soft tone. Gratitude shone in the MLA's eyes as he clasped my hands.

"Medicine is full of storms," I said, choosing my words carefully. "We don't control the wind: we adjust the sails. Mr. Manjunath, there's something important we must all hold on to in times of despair."

"And what might that be, Doctor?" asked Mr. Manjunath.

Shabnam interjected with a knowing smile,

"It's called hope and faith."

3

CHAPTER 3

Life shrinks or expands in proportion to one's courage.

–Anais Nin

Practicing clinical medicine is a journey fraught with challenges and profound learning experiences. Each patient presents a unique narrative, a tapestry woven with threads of hope, resilience, and sometimes, heart-wrenching struggle. There are some ideal patients who follow medical advice with unwavering dedication, their trust in their caregivers absolute. Yet, there are others whose paths are tangled by fear, denial, or circumstance, their compliance a labyrinth that tests a doctor's skill, patience, and empathy. Behind every "difficult" patient lies a story—a reason buried beneath layers of pain or misunderstanding. To guide such individuals toward healing often demands more than just textbook knowledge; it requires a transformative approach, a bridge built between science and the human spirit.

"Doctor, we are unable to handle her," Mrs. Vanaja sobbed, her voice trembling as she clutched the edge of my desk. Her eyes, red-rimmed from sleepless nights, mirrored the exhaustion of a mother grappling with helplessness. Behind her, through the glass partition of the MICU, lay her 14-year-old daughter, Renuka, frail and listless, her IV line a stark reminder of her fragility.

This marked Renuka's third admission in six months. Her diagnosis of Type 1 Diabetes had arrived like a thunderclap six months prior, shattering the ordinary rhythm of their lives. Once a spirited girl with a laugh that echoed through school corridors, Renuka now seemed a shadow of herself. The autoimmune assault on her pancreas had rendered her dependent on insulin, a lifeline she resisted with every fiber of her being.

"She refuses the injections," Mrs. Vanaja continued, her voice breaking. "She hides her insulin pens, skips meals, or binges on sweets—anything to pretend this isn't happening. We've sold jewelry, borrowed money… but how long can we keep doing this?" Her words hung heavy, a testament to the financial and emotional toll of Renuka's relapses.

I recalled the day we diagnosed Renuka. I had counseled both Renuka and her parents about the nature of the illness, its treatment, and the necessary precautions. It took some time for her parents to understand and accept their daughter's disease. However, it was more difficult with Renuka. She was a chirpy, bubbly girl who loved chocolates, ice creams, and sweets, and she was not willing to give up any of these. Moreover, she was afraid of injections and was not keen on taking insulin. Her non-compliance with dietary advice and insulin therapy led to her frequent hospitalizations.

Later, as I stood by Renuka's bedside, her gaze fixed on the ceiling, I searched for the right words. The hum of monitors filled the silence.

"Renuka, you must take your condition seriously. Ignoring your treatment will only land you back here," I urged gently.

"Why me, Doctor? What did I do wrong?" she asked, her innocence palpable.

"You've done nothing wrong. And diabetes isn't a punishment—it's a challenge life handed you. Like a difficult level in a video game. You need the right tools to conquer it."

"Have you ever sacrificed something you love, Doctor?"

"Indeed, I have. It ultimately made me a better person."

"How can you let go of something you like?"

"Sometimes, we must relinquish the good for the greater good. It's tough, but you must try earnestly."

"I can't accept this. My life feels ruined."

"No, Renuka. Don't give up on your dreams. God would not test you if He felt that you were incapable of this challenge."

Despite my earnest efforts to counsel her, she seemed too depressed to take in any guidance. I knew I needed to discover a method to bolster her confidence. Her resistance was a wall I couldn't scale alone. Reflecting on my other patients who faced similar struggles, I remembered one in particular who could be instrumental in assisting me. I knew what I had to do.

*****

Over the next few days, Shabnam and her team worked intensely to stabilize Renuka's condition.

"How's she doing?" I inquired.

"Remarkably well! Her outlook has completely transformed," Shabnam replied, her voice tinged with awe.

"What do you mean?"

"When she arrived, she was despondent. Now, she's vibrant and hopeful."

"I knew it would work!" I exclaimed, a surge of satisfaction warming my chest.

Shabnam frowned. "Knew what would work?"

"Swetha's arrival. It's made all the difference."

"Swetha? Who's Swetha?"

"Remember the young girl we treated years ago? The one with symptoms identical to Renuka's?"

"Oh, yes—she was critically ill. I haven't heard of her since."

"That's her."

Shabnam crossed her arms. "Rehan, how could someone from the past impact Renuka's situation now?"

Before I could answer, my phone buzzed. Reception was calling: the outpatient clinic was overflowing, and patients were growing restless.

"We'll discuss this later," I said, already halfway to the door. "Duty calls."

As I hurried away, I couldn't suppress a smile. The plan had succeeded beyond expectations.

Days later, Renuka stood at the hospital entrance, arm-in-arm with her mother, Mrs. Vanaja. Sunlight streamed through the windows, catching the quiet resolve in Renuka's eyes and the cautious hope softening her mother's weary face.

Keep fighting, I thought, watching them leave. The road ahead would be grueling, but her newfound resilience—that fragile spark of will—might just be the lifeline she needed.

*****

On World Diabetes Day, November 14, six months had passed. We organized an event emphasizing childhood diabetes awareness, inviting a select group of our Type 1 diabetic patients, including Renuka. She was now compliant with her medications, and her blood sugar levels were well controlled.

The event commenced with my overview of childhood diabetes prevalence, impact, and management. Shabnam discussed the vital precautions and monitoring necessary for diabetes care. The CEO concluded the program, speaking on our collective efforts against diabetes. Nearing the end of his address, he stated,

"I now announce the Young Achiever of the Year Award. Our recipient is a resilient young patient who was diagnosed with juvenile diabetes a few years ago. She has valiantly battled diabetes without letting it extinguish her dreams," the CEO announced, turning towards me.

"Ladies and gentlemen, I invite Dr. Rehan to present this award to a patient whose spirit and courage are indomitable—Ms. Swetha."

Shabnam glanced at me inquisitively and whispered, "Rehan, isn't she the one who influenced Renuka's perspective?"

With a knowing smile, I ascended the stage to present the award to Swetha.

"It is with great pleasure that I present this award to Swetha. Once burdened with sadness and the weight of her diagnosis, she has now rebounded with remarkable strength to conquer diabetes. Today, she takes a significant stride towards her future. Congratulations, Swetha, on your transformative journey from patient to aspiring doctor."

Swetha, much like Renuka, was diagnosed with Type 1 diabetes during her 10th standard. However, unlike Renuka, she approached her diagnosis differently. Swetha quickly accepted her condition and recovered, allowing herself to chase her dream of becoming a doctor. Swetha's determination never wavered. She studied diligently and excelled in her medical entrance examination, earning an impressive rank. After securing her rank, she visited me alongside her father. It was heartwarming and a source of immense pride for all of us. Soon, she would become a doctor herself. It was a story that would inspire anyone. When Swetha agreed to meet Renuka upon my request, she made a profound impression on her. Swetha became her symbol of hope.

As I handed the memento to Swetha, the room erupted in applause. I could see from a distance that the loudest cheers in the crowd came from Renuka.

In my closing speech, I shared their story, and concluded, "Medicine doesn't heal in a vacuum. Sometimes, it takes a survivor's spark to light another's way."

After the event, Shabnam came to me and asked,

"You planned this all along, didn't you? It was your strategy all along to introduce Renuka to Swetha—it revolutionized her outlook."

"Yes, Shabnam. It helped Renuka find her purpose and inspiration."

"Sometimes," I replied, "the best prescription isn't a pill: it's proof that someone like them thrived."

We are all broken in some way, but if we believe in ourselves, there is still enough stardust within us to perform a little magic!

CHAPTER 4

The night sinks into my bones,
the wind blows through me,
as I stand in the graveyard of our memories,
I'm haunted by a ghost that only I can see.

–Christy Ann Martine

Like any couple, we'd weathered our share of storms—misunderstandings that lingered like fog, disagreements that crackled like summer lightning, and silences that stretched taut as piano wires. Yet each trial, however sharp, had polished the edges of our bond, smoothing it into something resilient. Still, there was one incident that etched itself into our shared history, a raw testament to how swiftly emotions could unravel the seams of even the strongest love, or stitch them tighter than before.

It was a rain-soaked evening, the kind where the sky wept ceaselessly, turning roads into mirrored labyrinths and the world into a watercolor of grays. I'd just returned from an urgent call at Hope Ray Hospital, my clothes clinging to me like a second skin, the chill of the night seeping into my bones. Shabnam stood in the doorway of our modest living room, her silhouette framed by the amber glow of a table lamp, arms crossed tightly over her chest—a posture that betrayed her simmering worry.

"Rehan, what was the emergency this time?" she asked, her voice softer than the rain pattering against the windows, yet edged with a tension I knew all too well. She stepped forward, her feet soundless on the worn Persian rug, and handed me a towel. Her fingers brushed mine, fleeting and warm, a contrast to the damp cold that enveloped me.

I peeled off my drenched coat, the fabric heavy with rainwater, and sighed. She fretted over these late-night calls. Our home lay a distance from Hope Ray Hospital, and the thought of me driving through the nocturnal stillness unsettled her. Faithfully, she'd await my return each night.

"A suicide attempt, Rat poison" I said, running a hand through my tousled hair.

Shabnam's breath hitched, her dark eyes widening. "Why would she resort to that?"

"Shabnam," I began cautiously, "why assume it's a woman?"

She turned away, her gaze drifting to the window where raindrops streaked the glass like tears. "You know why, Rehan," she murmured. "In this city, in this world—it's always the women who swallow their pain until it poisons them." Her voice trembled, not with anger, but with a grief that echoed years of witnessing friends, neighbors, even her own mother bear the weight of silent suffering.

"True, they're sometimes more susceptible to emotional turmoil," I agreed.

"It must be her husband's fault," Shabnam declared, a hint of judgment in her tone.

Radhika, the patient, had arrived at the hospital lethargic, her husband a portrait of distress. He recounted a trivial quarrel, his pleas for her survival echoing in my ears.

"Shabnam, we're not here to pass judgment. Our duty is to heal and care," I reminded her.

"Alright, let's not argue. Time will reveal the truth," She whispered finally, echoing the words we both clung to in moments like these.

The following day, Radhika's condition had deteriorated. Shabnam and her team fought valiantly against the encroaching shadows of respiratory failure, shock, and hemorrhage. Rat poison's lethal grip held a grim prognosis.

"Rehan, she's declining. She needs life support," Shabnam reported, her voice heavy with the weight of the situation.

"Go ahead, Shabnam. We must do all we can. Her husband is shattered—they have a young child."

"And the rest of their family?"

"They're alone. It was a love marriage; they're estranged from their kin."

"How ironic—a love marriage leading to this. The mysteries of the heart are boundless…"

"Shabnam, sometimes it's a moment of impulse that tips the scales."

"Sometimes an impulse isn't just an impulse, Rehan. Sometimes it's the last cry of a drowning soul."

Shabnam still presumed that husband was at fault.

I stepped outside to converse with the patient's husband. He was a tall, slender man with unkempt hair and a somber look that suggested he hadn't slept all night.

"Doctor, please save Radhika. I cannot imagine life without her," he implored with a quivering voice.

"Mr. Laxman, she is in a critical and unstable condition, but rest assured, we are doing everything we can," I responded, offering him a glimmer of hope.

Near the reception desk, two police officers hovered, their khaki uniforms starched into rigid authority. The taller one thumbed a notepad, his boot tapping an impatient rhythm, while his partner—a woman with a tight bun and eyes like flint—scanned the room.

"Can I assist you?" I asked, stepping between them and the ICU's glass partition.

"Doctor, we need to take a statement from Mrs. Radhika regarding the poisoning incident," one officer stated.

"I'm sorry, but the patient is currently unable to provide any information. You may return once her condition stabilizes," I explained, detailing Radhika's precarious health.

At that moment, a commotion erupted: a guttural shout followed by the clatter of a metal chart hitting the floor.

A wiry man in a mud-spattered dhoti barreled toward us, his face a contorted mask of grief and rage.

"Hai Bhagwan!" He thrust a gnarled finger at Laxman, who shrank back as if struck and said, "Sir, there is no need to question Radhika. This man, Laxman, is to blame for her condition. My daughter married him against our wishes. Look at what he has done to her!" he exclaimed.

Laxman, taken aback by his father-in-law's outburst, silently left the scene. I couldn't help but feel a pang of sympathy for him.

The officers exchanged a glance, their zeal dampened by the raw theatre of human ruin.

"Return later," I said quietly.

A couple of days passed, and there was no noticeable improvement in Radhika's condition. Laxman remained a constant presence outside the ICU, eagerly awaiting updates on his wife's health. Approximately 72 hours later, Radhika began showing signs of recovery: her blood pressure stabilized, and her respiratory function improved. The medical team prepared to wean her off the ventilator. Eager to share the good news, I searched for her husband, but Laxman was nowhere to be found that day.

We proceeded with extubating Radhika.

"Radhika, how do you feel now?" Shabnam asked gently.

"I want to see my husband," she replied in a faint, trembling voice.

"We'll bring him here," Shabnam reassured her, glancing at me.

"Please call him immediately…" Radhika pleaded again.

"What happened, Radhika?" Shabnam pressed, unable to contain her curiosity.

"It's all my fault. We're from a middle-class family and we married against our parents' wishes. We have no one else. My husband saves every penny he earns and entrusts it to me. Against his advice, I enrolled our son in a prestigious school and invested all our savings in a private chit fund…" Radhika's voice broke as tears streamed down her face.

"It's okay, Radhika. We can discuss this later," I interrupted, worried about her fragile state.

"I lost all his hard-earned money. The chit fund was a fraud. When I told him, he was devastated but said nothing. Overwhelmed by guilt, I… I took the poison," she confessed, her sobs echoing through the room.

Radhika's confession stunned us. She had impulsively ingested rat poison after losing all their savings to a fraudulent chit fund. While everyone assumed Laxman was to blame, the truth was far more complex. Yet, amid the turmoil, he remained silent, bearing the weight of accusations. I felt compelled to reach out to him, to reassure him that the situation would soon resolve. I tried to locate Laxman but found no trace of him. Calls to his mobile went unanswered. Had fear driven him to flee?

The following morning, I encountered Mr. Ramana, a close friend of Laxman's, who arrived at the hospital with Laxman's son accompanying him. Concerned, I asked about Laxman's whereabouts. Mr. Ramana explained that Laxman had entrusted his son to him, claiming he needed to stay at the hospital. However, after failing to reach Laxman for over 24 hours, Mr. Ramana had come seeking answers himself. Laxman's sudden disappearance was alarming: his anxious wife awaited his return, his son lingered at the hospital, and Laxman himself had vanished without explanation. Where could he have gone? The question hung in the air—a haunting, unsolved mystery.

Later that day, Mr. Anand, the hospital administrator, summoned Shabnam and me for an urgent meeting. Upon entering his office, we were greeted by a police officer.

"Dr. Rehan, this is Mr. Satya Kumar, the Sub-Inspector of Police," Mr. Anand said.

After exchanging greetings, the inspector cut straight to the chase.

"Doctor, I'm here regarding your patient, Mrs. Radhika. How is she doing?"

"She's recovering and out of danger. We're waiting for her husband," I replied.

The inspector's expression darkened.

"Dr. Rehan, there's been a tragic development."

"What happened?" I asked, dread tightening in my chest.

"We found Laxman dead in his apartment. He'd hanged himself from the ceiling."

I froze, speechless. Shabnam stood equally stunned beside me.

"He left a suicide note," the inspector continued. "Dr. Rehan, it's addressed to you." He handed me the letter.

The revelation blindsided me. Had the weight of false accusations shattered him? Why me? With trembling hands, I unfolded the note. It read…

Dr. Rehan,

My love for Radhika is pure and eternal. Nothing will ever change that. But she chose to end her life, leaving me behind. With her by my side, I could fight for anything. Without her, life has no meaning for me. We sacrificed everything for each other. I cannot bear the thought that I might have been somehow responsible for her critical condition. The world blames me, but God knows the truth.

If you miraculously save her, please tell her I have always loved her above all else. If she passes away, we will meet in a place where only our love remains.

My son is the legacy of our love. Let him stay with Radhika as a memory of me, or may he find shelter and affection with his doting grandfather.

I hold no one accountable for my death.

Laxman

The letter laid bare the depth of Laxman's despair. He had chosen death's silence over a world that refused to understand his love. I couldn't bring myself to shatter Radhika with the truth, so with a trembling resolve, I asked Shabnam to deliver the crushing news. Their story—a tempest of devotion and sacrifice—had reached its sorrowful end.

"Shabnam," I said quietly, "do you understand now the depths to which love can drive us?"

Her voice softened with regret. "I do. I judged too harshly. Their story wasn't devoid of love. It was the courage to endure together that they lacked."

"Then promise me," I urged, "that no storm, however fierce, will ever divide us."

"Always," she whispered.

Love, I thought, is a fire kindled by the heart: it warms, it guides, but left untamed, it devours everything in its wake.

Chapter 5

*You cannot swim for new
horizons until you have
courage to lose sight of the shore.*

–William Faulkner

After our marriage, finding time for a honeymoon or holiday was a challenge. Both of us had to time it perfectly. Either I was occupied with sick patients, or Shabnam had her own struggles in the ICU. Shabnam had always wanted to see the snow-clad mountains of Switzerland. I thought it was a perfect getaway. When we finally secured some patient-free time during the winter off-season, I decided to plan a Swiss holiday.

"Hi Aradhana, can you plan a short holiday to Switzerland for us?" I explained our travel dates to my Cox & Kings tour operator.

She took some time and called back.

"I can customize a Swiss tour for you, but there's a glitch," she said.

"What is it? Don't worry about the cost of the package," I replied, not wanting to miss the opportunity.

"It's not the flights or the cost. The cable car to Mount Titlis is closed due to heavy snowfall. You can still visit other sites like Lucerne, Bern, Zurich, and Interlaken."

"Switzerland without Mount Titlis is nothing!" I exclaimed in despair. "Shabnam won't like this. I'll get back to you."

Later that day, I discussed it with Shabnam.

"It's a bummer. We hardly get a chance to go anywhere, and now this happens," she said disappointedly.

We shared the failed plan with Dad and Mom. After listening to me, Dad said,

"Sometimes we miss good things because better things are in store."

"Hmm… Did you ever want to see something badly but couldn't?" I asked casually.

"Yes. I always wanted to go to Kashmir with your mother, but couldn't for one reason or another."

The situation in Kashmir was often volatile due to militant activities, and the media consistently portrayed it as a dangerous travel destination.

The next morning, I dialed Aradhana, my pulse quickening with resolve. "What if we pivot to Kashmir instead of Switzerland?"

A pause. "Of course," she replied cautiously, "but you're aware of the… risks?"

"Fully aware." My grip tightened on the phone. "Some chances are worth taking."

"Alright, I'll secure a tour for two—"

"Four," I cut in, warmth flooding my voice. "This is my chance to fulfill my father's long-cherished dream—I won't let it slip away."

*****

We embarked on our journey to Kashmir with equal parts of excitement and apprehension. However, our fears dissolved as we explored the region. The serene houseboats of Srinagar, with their soothing shikara rides on Dal Lake; Gulmarg's panoramic vistas; Son Marg's snow-capped peaks and meadows; and Pahal gam's lush green Basiran Valley—all left us awestruck. The people were warm and hospitable, enduring hardships with resilience. Tourism was a major source of their livelihood, and exaggerated media reports had severely impacted it.

As our embroidered shikara glided across Dal Lake's mirror-like surface at dusk, the mountains' reflection trembling in the ripples, my father's composure cracked. He stared at my mother, the golden light softening his wrinkles, and whispered, "I'd stopped believing this day would exist."

My mother, Farida, squeezed his hand. Her Kashmiri saffron scarf catching the breeze, and she murmured, "Surreal, isn't it? A lifetime's dream… fulfilled."

I'd visited Switzerland before, but Kashmir was an entirely different realm—raw, untamed, alive. Standing atop a viewpoint in Sonmarg, Shabnam gripped my arm, her voice trembling with awe. "This is breathtaking. We chase foreign skies while overlooking the emerald in our own backyard. This is paradise—undisputed, unscripted. Missing Switzerland was destiny's nudge.'"

I gazed at the horizon, where snow met sky. "Agreed. Sometimes detours lead us home."

While returning home, a security guard at the airport asked,

"Did you enjoy this paradise on Earth?"

"Of course, it was an amazing trip," I replied honestly.

"When you return home, pray for us. Pray it doesn't become paradise lost," he said with genuine concern.

*****

Our flight from Srinagar to Hyderabad had a layover in Delhi. We boarded the evening flight to Hyderabad, refreshed and rejuvenated, having disconnected entirely from hospital duties.

As we approached the Hyderabad airport, a scream echoed through the cabin.

"It's an emergency!"

My heart raced, fearing something was wrong with the plane. Shabnam and I exchanged tense glances.

"Is there a doctor on board?" the flight attendant shouted. "A passenger needs help!"

Shabnam and I raised our hands and rushed to the man. He was an elderly, unresponsive male. The flight attendant promptly provided us a medical kit. While I gathered his medical history from his wife, Shabnam checked his vitals using the blood pressure apparatus and pulse oximeter. The patient was diabetic, had taken his medications, but had erratic food intake. He had grown weak and drowsy, emitting groaning sounds.

"His vitals are stable. Unlikely to be cardiac. He's moving all limbs," Shabnam declared.

"It could be hypoglycemia. Shabnam, obtain IV access. Look for 50% dextrose in the kit," I instructed.

"Is there a glucometer here?"

"No," Shabnam replied, shaking her head.

"Does anyone have a glucometer? A blood glucose monitor?" I called out.

A middle-aged man stepped forward. "I have one!"

The reading showed 40 mg/dl, a clear case of hypoglycemic encephalopathy. The patient had developed low blood sugar, which affected his brain, leading to an unresponsive state. However, it was completely reversible if identified and corrected in time. Shabnam secured an intravenous line and administered 50% dextrose. Within minutes, the patient woke up, alert and responsive.

"Emergency resolved! Thanks to Dr. Rehan and Dr. Shabnam!" the captain announced. The cabin erupted in applause.

Back in our seats, Shabnam laughed softly. "Duty never clocks out."

I squeezed her hand. "Or maybe it follows where we're needed most."

Kashmir had gifted us more than vistas. It mirrored our purpose. Amid snow-draped valleys and an unexpected crisis at 30,000 feet, we rediscovered the thread binding us: two healers, forever entwined by calling and chance.

As Hyderabad's lights twinkled below, I finally understood my father's words. The "better things" were not places, but moments—unplanned, imperfect, and utterly ours.

6

CHAPTER 6

We can't heal the world today.
But we can begin with a voice
of compassion, a heart of love
and an act of kindness.

–Mary Davis

Hope Ray Hospital had always been more than just brick and mortar. It was a living, breathing entity, its corridors humming with stories of resilience and redemption. Founded in 1995 by Dr. Ravi Ray, a surgeon disillusioned by the commercialization of healthcare, the institution was built on a radical premise: "No life is negotiable." Over the years, it had grown from a 50-bed facility into a sprawling network of care, its green-and-white emblem now synonymous with integrity in a landscape of profit-driven hospitals.

Hope Ray Hospital had blossomed from a modest regional facility into a beacon of healthcare excellence, its reputation now stretching beyond state lines. With blueprints to establish branches in Maharashtra, Karnataka, and Telangana, the institution was poised to bring its unique ethos "Healing with Humanity", to millions. "We're not building franchises," Dr. Anand, the administrator, often reminded the staff. "We're planting seeds of trust." This philosophy trickled down to every department. Nurses were trained to spend an extra five minutes holding the hand of a frightened patient; janitors discreetly slipped fruit to families who couldn't afford cafeteria meals. It was this invisible tapestry of compassion that made Hope Ray Hospital extraordinary, and Dr. Raj Kiran its brightest thread.

Among the star consultants was Dr. Raj Kiran, our dedicated cardiologist. A titan in cardiology, he was as much a legend for his skill as for his sorrow. His late wife, Anjali, had been his counterbalance, her laughter a salve to his intensity. They'd met in medical school, where she'd teased him for his "obsession with heartbeats" until he'd retorted, "Someone has to keep yours steady." Their marriage was a whirlwind—picnics in rainstorms, midnight debates about ethics, and a shared dream of opening a rural clinic.

All of it ended on a highway slick with monsoon rain. Anjali, seven months pregnant, had been rushing to deliver a premature baby when a truck swerved into her lane. Dr. Raj Kiran arrived at the accident scene to find her still clutching her stethoscope, her body curled protectively over her abdomen. He never spoke of that night, but the hospital grapevine claimed he'd performed CPR on her for an hour, his screams blending with the thunder, until his colleagues pried him away.

Now, he lived in a spartan apartment close to the hospital. Left with only memories and his stethoscope, Dr. Raj Kiran had buried his grief in his work, transforming the Cardiac Intensive Care Unit (CICU) into a sanctuary of second chances. Colleagues often joked that he'd married the hospital itself. His days began before dawn and ended long after midnight, his office walls adorned not with family photos but with letters from patients whose lives he'd salvaged. To me, he was both mentor and cautionary tale: a man who'd turned his pain into a superpower, yet bore its weight in the shadows beneath his eyes.

*****

It was a sweltering Saturday when Ashok's call shattered my afternoon calm. Ashok, my childhood friend, had a knack for roping me into favors. "Rehan, I need you to see someone," he pleaded. "Mr. Shastri—a temple priest—has been vomiting all morning. He's broke, Rehan. Minimal tests, okay?"

I agreed, though unease prickled my neck. Indigestion? Priests rarely complained unless pain clawed through their stoicism.

By 4 PM, Mr. Shastri hobbled into the ER, his face ashen beneath the fluorescent lights. A portly man in his late 50s, he clutched his dhoti with trembling hands, each step labored. His wife, a slight woman draped in a faded sari, hovered nervously beside him, her eyes darting between the monitors and my face.

"Upper abdominal pain… indigestion…" he mumbled, doubling over as a fresh wave of nausea hit. The nurse, Priya, swooped in, her practiced hands capturing his vitals. Her brow furrowed. "BP 90/60, pulse 48," she murmured.

Too low. Too slow.

I pressed my fingers to his clammy wrist. "Any chest pain? Breathlessness?"

He shook his head. "Only… burning here." His hand drifted to his sternum.

Gastritis, I told myself. But why the bradycardia, the slow heart rate? My mind raced through differentials—bleeding ulcer? Electrolyte imbalance? Then the cardiac monitor's rhythmic beeping snagged my attention. The ST segment in Lead II wasn't just elevated; it was skyrocketing, a jagged mountain range on the screen.

Inferior wall MI? A possible heart attack?

Before I could react, a voice sliced through the chaos.

"Prep the Cath lab. Now."

Dr. Raj Kiran stood in the doorway, his white coat immaculate, eyes locked on the ECG. In three strides, he was at the bedside, his fingers already palpating Mr. Shastri's femoral pulse. "Aspirin 325 mg, stat. Nitroglycerin spray. Page the Cath team."

The diagnosis struck me like a defibrillator shock. Shastri's "Indigestion" was a heart attack in disguise, a cruel masquerade. Dr. Raj Kiran's hand clamped my shoulder, steadying me.

"Classic presentation in diabetics," he said, not unkindly. "In Inferior wall MI, pain radiates to the epigastrium. Remember that."

The priest's wife whispered, "Hai Ram, what's happening?"

Dr. Raj Kiran turned to her, his tone softening. "Your husband's heart is tired. We need to help it." He didn't say heart attack—not yet. Not until he'd armored her with hope.

Chaos erupted. Nurses scrambled; crash carts rattled. But Dr. Raj Kiran remained an island of calm. He knelt beside Mr. Shastri, cupping the man's sweat-slicked face. "We'll take care of you," he promised, his voice a balm. The priest's wife crumpled into a chair, her sobs muffling the beep of IV pumps.

Then came the hurdle: money. Cardiac catheterization, stents, ICU stay—the tally would exceed ₹1.5 lakh. Ashok's warning echoed in my head. I pulled Dr. Raj Kiran aside, guilt souring my tongue.

"Sir, he can't afford…"

For a heartbeat, his mask slipped. A flicker of pain—or memory? —crossed his face. Then he straightened. "Pro bono. We will clear it with Dr. Anand."

*****

The procedure was a ballet of precision. A 90% blockage in the right coronary artery. Dr. Raj Kiran navigated the occluded artery with the grace of a maestro, deploying a stent that bloomed like a life-saving flower. By dawn, Mr. Shastri had stabilized, his wife now wearing a smile of relief.

Ashok visited the next day, disbelief etched across his face. "A corporate hospital waiving fees? You've rewritten the rulebook, Rehan."

"The credit belongs entirely to Dr. Raj Kiran. He's a wonderful soul," I replied.

But the true revelation came a week later, at discharge. Mr. Shastri's wife—her name was Lakshmi—stood in Dr. Raj Kiran's office, flanked by her daughters.

Tearfully, she addressed Dr. Raj Kiran,

"Sir, I've come to express my heartfelt thanks and regards for your generosity. Mr. Shastri means everything to us. You haven't just saved him; you've saved our entire family."

Dr. Raj Kiran offered a gentle smile. "I was simply doing my duty. He's meant to remain by your side for many years to come. Cherish him dearly."

Clutching a delicate box, the woman pressed on, her voice trembling. "I know I can never truly repay your kindness, but please accept this humble token from our family." She extended the gift toward him, her hands steady despite her emotion.

Initially surprised, Dr. Raj Kiran hesitated but eventually accepted the gift upon my insistence. The lady left with her daughters, their smiles reflecting deep gratitude.

"Sir, won't you open the gift?" I ventured gently.

Dr. Raj Kiran lifted the box lid, his face softening into quiet melancholy. After a pause, he extended it toward me. "Do not take this amiss," he said, his voice steady but subdued. "Keep it for my sake, and give it to Shabnam."

Bewildered, I peered inside: nestled in velvet lay a pair of intricately crafted gold ear studs and a folded slip of paper. Unfolding it, I read the handwritten words: "Thank you, Doctor. These are for your wife."

In that moment, we all felt the ghost of Anjali—her laughter, her absence, the void she'd left. Words failed me. Dr. Raj Kiran, whose home had stood empty since his wife's passing, stared vacantly into the distance. The gift—a gesture of gratitude meant for a woman long gone—hung between us like an unanswered prayer. With solemn understanding, I cradled it in my hands, its delicate weight now a testament to both his loss and my quiet resolve to honor it.

*****

That night, I found Shabnam on our terrace, her silhouette framed by the monsoon clouds. She turned the ear studs in her palm, their gold catching the dim light.

"They're beautiful," she whispered, her voice a frayed thread of wonder. "Like starlight forged into earth."

I told her everything—Lakshmi's tears, Dr. Raj Kiran's quiet storm, the cruel irony of a gift meant for a ghost. Shabnam's eyes welled, but her voice stayed steady. She clasped the studs, not to her ears, but to her heart.

"They're not mine to keep," she decided. Opening her jewelry box, she nestled the studs beside her grandmother's pearls. "We'll save them. For our daughter, someday. So, she'll know kindness has a lineage."

As the first raindrops fell, I realized Dr. Raj Kiran's legacy wasn't in the lives he'd saved, but in the compassion, he'd ignited—a flame that would outlast us all.

CHAPTER 7

*The hands that rocked your cradle
now tremble in silence. Hold them
before they still forever.*

–Anonymous

Providing medical care for elderly patients carries significant challenges due to the diverse health issues they face. Often, these patients struggle to articulate their symptoms clearly. Many withhold their concerns, unwilling to burden their children. Others live apart from their children, who may reside in different cities, states, or even abroad. Despite these complexities, elderly patients often trust their doctors with secrets they hesitate to share even with their own families.

I once treated an elderly couple, Mr. Janakiram and Mrs. Sumathi, who visited me monthly for diabetes and hypertension management. In their seventies, they were a devoted pair, always caring for one another. Mr. Janakiram, 78, and Mrs. Sumathi, 75, had been married for nearly five decades. Theirs was a love story forged in simpler times. He was a retired school principal with a passion for Carnatic music, while she was a former literature teacher who could recite Tamil poetry by heart.

Their monthly visits to me were rituals of camaraderie. They arrived hand-in-hand, their synchronized routines a testament to decades of partnership. Mr. Janakiram would meticulously note his wife's blood sugar readings in a weathered journal, while Mrs. Sumathi fretted over his salt intake. Yet, their conversations never broached the absence of their children.

One humid afternoon, as I reviewed Mrs. Sumathi's stable HbA1c levels, I ventured a question that had lingered in my mind. "Sir, I've never seen your children accompany you. Do they not stay nearby?"

Mr. Janakiram's smile wavered. "Both are in America, Doctor. Rajesh is an engineer in Houston; Saritha teaches in Boston."

"Do they visit often?"

Mrs. Sumathi interjected softly, "They last came five years ago for Diwali. Flights are costly, and their leaves are scarce." Her voice carried no reproach, only resignation.

I pressed gently, "And you? Have you considered visiting them?"

The couple exchanged a glance. "We went once," Mr. Janakiram replied. "When Saritha's first child was born. But we felt… out of place. Their lives are hectic. We didn't want to intrude."

The subtext hung heavy: We were guests in our own children's homes.

"Don't you miss them?"

"Every day," he admitted, his voice trembling. "But we want them to thrive. Their happiness is enough for us."

My heart ached for them. They'd sacrificed their prime years to raise their children, only to face old age alone. The couple's modest home in Secunderabad, once vibrant with family gatherings, now echoed with the silence of empty rooms and unanswered hopes.

*****

One day, Mr. Janakiram called urgently. "Doctor, Sumathi is unwell. I'm bringing her to the hospital."

Mrs. Sumathi arrived in the ER, semiconscious, with critically high blood sugar and blood pressure.

"What happened?" I asked her husband.

"She didn't wake this morning," he said, panic edging his words. "She was drowsy, making strange sounds. Her glucose was very high. Will she recover?"

"We'll run tests, including a CT scan to check for stroke. Was she taking her medication regularly?"

He hesitated. "I found her pills untouched. She stopped them weeks ago."

"Why would she do that?" I asked, surprised.

"Two weeks back," he murmured, tears welling, "she begged our children to visit for our 50th anniversary. They refused, citing work. She sank into despair. I tried comforting her, but... she shut me out."

"I'm so sorry," I said. "We'll do all we can."

The CT scan of Mrs. Sumathi confirmed the worst: a massive ischemic stroke, her brain's left hemisphere ravaged. We moved her to the MICU, but her prognosis was grim. I urged Mr. Janakiram to inform their children.

The next day, their daughter Saritha called from New York.

"Doctor," she snapped, "Mother was under your care. How could you let this happen? Aren't you monitoring them?" Her accusatory tone masked her panic.

Stunned by her rude tone, I replied, "Ask your father why she stopped her medication." I handed the phone back, disheartened.

Mr. Janakiram apologized. "Forgive her, Doctor. She's distraught. You've been our anchor. Ignore her words."

Shabnam, witnessing the exchange, remarked, "Classic 'Daughter from California' syndrome."

"What's that?"

"A term for absent relatives who suddenly demand aggressive care out of guilt," she explained. "They're in denial, blaming doctors instead of facing their own neglect."

"How true," I agreed. "Guilt morphs into aggression and fuels their impractical demands."

As Mrs. Sumathi's consciousness continued to deteriorate, we had no choice but to perform an endotracheal intubation, securing her airway and placing her on mechanical ventilation. The rhythmic whoosh of the ventilator filled the room, a cold contrast to the human tragedy unfolding around it. I stepped into the hallway to call her husband, bracing myself for the conversation ahead.

Mr. Janakiram arrived within minutes, his face ashen and hands trembling. When I explained her critical condition—the stroke's irreversible damage, the machines now sustaining her—he crumpled into the chair beside her bed, his voice cracking like glass.

"Dr. Rehan," he choked out, staring at his wife's motionless form, "she has been my shadow for fifty monsoons. My morning tea, my evening walks… How does one breathe when half their soul is gone?" He paused, wiping his spectacles with a frayed handkerchief. "Forgive me, Doctor. I know this is no time for… but my son, Rajesh, insists on speaking with you. I told him not to trouble you, but…" His words dissolved into silence, the unspoken plea hanging between us.

Their son Rajesh then called, asking, "Should I fly to India?"

"She's critical. The choice is yours," I said, baffled that he needed prompting.

"Keep her alive until I arrive!" he pleaded.

"We'll try," I promised.

On their anniversary, Mr. Janakiram entered the MICU in a spotless white kurta, a vermillion sindoor packet in hand. Ignoring the beeping monitors, he traced a crimson line along his wife's forehead. "Happy anniversary, my dear," he whispered. "Remember our vows? 'Through joy and sorrow'…"

"She hears you," I said softly, gripping his shoulder.

Moments later, Rajesh stood at his mother's bedside, his arrival timed to the mechanical sigh of the ventilator. He hovered over her still form, his hands gripping the guardrail as if anchoring himself to a reality he could no longer recognize. The absence of her voice—the lack of even a flutter beneath paper-thin eyelids—left him stranded in a liminal space between regret and grief.

"Amma?" he whispered, the childhood endearment cracking like a dried seedpod.

The only response was the ventilator's metronomic reply.

How often do we squander a lifetime with parents, only to reunite at their deathbeds?

Mrs. Sumathi lingered for three more days. Her death certificate listed "cerebral infarction" as the cause, but I knew the truth: she'd succumbed to a broken heart.

Rajesh urged his father to move to America, but Mr. Janakiram refused.

"My life with her is here. Every corner of our home holds her voice. I won't abandon her memories." he insisted.

*****

Weeks dissolved into months without any sign of Mr. Janakiram at the OP clinic. His absence lingered like an unanswered question, gnawing at the edges of my routine. By the third missed appointment, I instructed my secretary to trace his whereabouts. The silence that followed felt less like coincidence and more like fate's grim punctuation.

I encountered Shabnam during lunch recess. Observing my somber mood, she inquired,

"Rehan, is everything okay?"

"Shabnam," I replied, "what could be more painful and worse than dying?" I posed the question back to her. Shabnam remained silent.

"It's dying alone."

Sadly, Mr. Janakiram passed away from a sudden cardiac arrest a month after his wife's demise-a solitary end to a love story etched in sacrifice and solitude.

In our relentless pursuit of progress, have we severed the sacred bonds that once transformed aging into a communal journey? Time, I've come to understand, is a currency heedlessly squandered by the young—a resource drained until it leaves the old impoverished.

8

CHAPTER 8

*I know of no higher fortitude than
stubbornness in the face
of overwhelming odds.*

–Louis Nizer

Courage is not a single note but a symphony, a complex harmony of fear, resolve, and vulnerability. It can thunder like a storm or whisper like a breeze, but its essence lies in its persistence. Life's most unscripted moments often become the crucible where true character is revealed, stripping away facades to expose the raw nerves beneath. Through three lives intertwined with mine, I learned that courage is not the absence of fear but the tenacity to move forward despite its weight.

Dr. Shekhar was a legend in our hospital, a surgeon whose reputation for tackling hopeless cases bordered on myth. He fearlessly accepted any case, even those that others would avoid. While some admired his courage, others felt envious.

I still remember the day he strode into the ICU to confront a 70-year-old man with a ruptured aortic aneurysm, a case three senior surgeons had declined.

"If I don't try, he dies tonight," he said, his voice strong as steel. "If I do, he might live. That's a chance I have to take."

The surgery lasted 11 hours. By the end, Dr. Shekhar's scrubs were drenched, his eyes bloodshot, but the patient's pulse held steady. Nurses exchanged glances of awe; consultants muttered about "reckless heroics." Dr. Shekhar thrived in this duality, admired and resented, a man who wore his invincibility like armor.

One day, I received an urgent call from the ER: "Dr. Rehan, please rush to the emergency room. Dr. Shekar, our surgeon, has collapsed and injured himself." I hurried to the ER, wondering what could have caused this strong man to collapse. When I burst into the bay, the scene defied logic. Shekhar lay flat on the gurney, his trademark crisp collar askew, yet his gaze burned with lucidity. We checked his vitals and ECG, and everything appeared normal.

"Sir, what happened?" I asked, as I palpated his neck for carotid deficits.

Dr. Shekhar's voice fractured, the words spilling out like shards of glass.

"Rehan, I recently underwent a routine health check. I had intended to discuss the results with you, but," His thumb jerked toward the X-ray viewer, trembling faintly, "that shadow in the right upper lobe... I've seen it a hundred times in others. I never imagined staring at my own lungs and... suddenly, the fear of cancer overwhelmed me." He trailed off, knuckles whitening around the gurney rail. "One moment I was calculating survival rates, stage probabilities, adjuvant therapy options. The next, I was on the floor, collapsed and injured myself."

"Oh, that's what happened? It could be just a vasovagal syncope," I said, forcing calm into the words. "Stress-induced fainting." I was a bit surprised by the sudden weakening of his mental fortitude. I hadn't expected him to be so emotionally vulnerable and fragile when it came to his own health.

"Rehan, do you think it's cancer? I don't smoke, but I've lost a few pounds of weight. I assumed it was due to my diet and exercise. I'm quite concerned. Could you please take a look and share your opinion?"

I reviewed all his test reports and X-rays. He had an opacity in the right upper lung, and I consulted with the radiologist. It appeared to be suggestive of pulmonary tuberculosis, a highly treatable and curable condition.

"Not malignancy," I told Dr. Shekhar, watching his surgeon's mind dissect the words. "Pulmonary TB, a curable invader. Six months of antitubercular drugs, and you'll be back to normal."

I started him on anti-TB medications and within a few months, he made a full recovery. However, this incident revealed to me, for the first time, how vulnerable he truly was. Here was a mortal who'd glimpsed the abyss and flinched—whose hands, steady when wielding a scalpel over others, shook while swallowing his own pills.

The surgeon's armor of invincibility had rusted through. What remained was something truer: an ordinary man who'd learned courage isn't the absence of fear, but the humility to acknowledge it. The courage he used to project in the past seemed absent.

*****

A few months later, I also witnessed something diametrically opposite. Dr. Wilson Thomas, our nephrologist, was a soft-spoken personality who quietly went about his work. Although he didn't interact much with us, his patients held him in high regard. His patients adored him not for grand gestures but for the way he'd sit at their bedsides, chart forgotten, as they unspooled fears about dialysis or dying. "Healing isn't just in the kidneys," he once told me. "It's in the pauses between words."

One day, he experienced sudden abdominal pain and had to be hospitalized. The diagnostic workup revealed shocking news: he had cancer of the large intestine. The hospital braced for fallout. How would our gentle nephrologist, a man who apologized for ordering extra tests, weather cancer's brutality? But Dr. Thomas surprised us all.

He responded with eerie calm.

The night before his surgery, he emailed me a spreadsheet of his patients' treatment plans, annotated with reminders like "Mrs. Gupta fears needles, use pediatric IVs."

When I visited him post-op, his face was pale, but his eyes sparkled. "They say I'll lose my hair," he mused, touching his thinning scalp. "I've always wanted an excuse to try baldness."

Chemotherapy hollowed him, shrinking his frame, leaching color from his olive-toned skin. Yet in that crucible of suffering, Dr. Thomas wielded his keyboard like a scalpel, dissecting his agony in a blog titled *'Notes from the Other Side'*. His prose transformed nausea into poetry ("a carousel spun by demons") and fatigue into existential metaphor ("swimming through amber while the world speeds by"). When he described neuropathy as "ghost ants marching beneath my skin," thousands of patients finally felt seen. The blog went viral not for its medical insights, but for its unflinching humanity. Thomas never called it bravery. "Just stitching my chaos into sentences," he'd say. But in those stitches, readers found a map to navigate their own darkness, and proof that even a ravaged body could house an unquenchable light.

When he returned to work, gaunt but radiant, the staff lined the corridors, clapping. He waved them off, embarrassed. "I'm just here to do my job," he insisted, but his presence had shifted something in us all.

Dr. Thomas had become a symbol of strength and fortitude in the hospital—the man who defeated cancer.

*****

But there is one story that no one would ever know—the story of a young duty medical officer. She was a beautiful, sincere, and dedicated young lady who hailed from a lower-middle-class family. Her father had suffered a paralytic stroke and was incapacitated. Being unmarried, she became the sole earning member of her family, and her job held immense importance for her.

One day, she came to my OP chamber and requested a consultation.

"Hi, Dr. Sneha, is everything fine?" I asked.

"Sir, I have a non-healing ulcer on the right side of my tongue," she replied, opening her mouth to reveal the area of concern. The ulcer was large, and according to Sneha, it had persisted for more than four weeks. Most aphthous ulcers are small and heal within a couple of weeks, but this one was different. Adjacent to the ulcer were sharp teeth, raising the possibility of cancer in an unhealing large ulcer on the tongue.

"Dr. Sneha, I believe it would be best to perform a biopsy. I recommend that you see our ENT surgeon and then report back to me," I advised her. Sneha left with a worried expression on her face.

Within a week, she returned with her biopsy report. The results confirmed it: cancer of the tongue.

I opened my mouth to shape the platitudes we both loathed—caught early, treatment protocols—but she spoke first, her diction precise as a scalpel's edge.

"Stage T2N0M0 based on imaging. I'll need hemi glossectomy with sentinel node biopsy. Dr. Menon's robotic surgery team, I presume?"

Her composure was clinical, chilling. She might have been discussing a patient's chart, not the impending amputation of her speech's instrument.

"Sneha, your parents—" I began, but she interjected.

"Sir, I understand what this means. I have a favor to ask."

"Sure, Sneha. How can I help?"

"I need you to keep this matter confidential. Please don't inform my parents. Additionally, I would appreciate Mr. Anand's support to maintain my job security and cover my treatment through insurance," she requested.

"Consider it done," I vowed, the words heavier than any informed consent I'd ever signed. My pen hovered over her treatment plan, its blue ink suddenly inadequate to capture what we both knew: This wasn't just about securing insurance codes or surgical slots. It was a pact to guard her fragile ecosystem, the ailing father, the siblings clinging to her paycheck, the PG dreams balanced atop this crumbling Jenga tower.

A year later, Sneha came to meet me with her mother. The woman before me bore little resemblance to the gaunt intern I'd last seen—cheekbones softened by regained weight, eyes luminous without the glaze of painkillers. She held a sweet box in her hands and wore a broad smile.

"Sir, I've come to resign. I wanted to meet you and express my gratitude before leaving," she said, her smile unwavering. I was taken aback. The job had been her lifeline. Why would she resign after all she had endured to keep it intact?

"But why are you leaving, Sneha?" I asked, genuinely surprised.

"Because I passed the postgraduate entrance examination and will soon begin my surgical training," she replied, offering the sweet box.

Sneha's battle against cancer, her unwavering determination, and her refusal to let her dreams fade away made her truly exceptional.

In the end, I realized that we don't conquer fear. We learn to carry it, and let it carve us into something unbreakable.

Chapter 9

*Tools such as compassion, trust, empathy, love, and
ethical discernment are already in our possession.
The next sensible step would be to use them.*

–Aberjhani

The patient-doctor relationship is a paradox: equal parts fragile and profound. When trust exists, patients surrender to care without hesitation, freeing us to act decisively, even in high-stakes scenarios. But with skeptical patients, every step becomes a battle. They dissect prescriptions on Google, demand second opinions, and scrutinize motives, haunted by past betrayals or innate distrust. While skepticism isn't inherently wrong, it shackles medicine's artistry. Defensive practice creeps in: we avoid risks, order unnecessary tests, and withhold bold treatments. The irony? Those who pride themselves on "outsmarting" doctors often sabotage their own care.

Yet for every doubting Thomas, there's a Mrs. Hameeda.

She arrived in the ICU with a raging urinary infection, her husband a Paradise Hotel chef. Between labored breaths, she bargained: "Get me well, Doctor, and I'll treat your team to Hyderabad's finest biryani."

I chuckled. "My team is… sizable."

She gradually recovered and returned home. A week later, I received a dekcha (traditional cooking pot) filled with delicious Hyderabadi biryani delivered to the canteen, accompanied by a note:

"Thank you, Dr. Rehan. This is for you and your team— Mrs. Hameeda."

We savored the scrumptious biryani, followed by Double Ka Meetha, a classic Hyderabadi dessert. Noticing the mobile number on the note, I called Mrs. Hameeda.

"Thank you! That was the best Hyderabadi biryani we've had in ages. Please thank your husband too!"

"Dr. Rehan, this isn't my husband's 'Paradise Biryani'. It's homemade, straight from my kitchen, infused with love and gratitude."

"Fabulous! You're an incredible cook!"

"And you," she replied warmly, "are a wonderful doctor."

Many such moments grace our clinical practice. A grateful son gifting a Tommy Hilfiger watch after his mother's recovery. A husband presenting a Samsung Tab when his wife overcame pneumonia. A farmer returning with baskets of fresh vegetables, still earthy from his fields. None of these gestures do we desire or like to accept, for our duty is to heal, never to expect gratitude in return.

But medicine's pendulum swings violently.

One evening, an elderly man shuffled in with back pain and lethargy—a diagnostic quagmire. The Orthopedic team suspected spinal decay; neurology cleared his brain scan. Only his soaring ESR hinted trouble. A spinal tap ruled out infection but he soon became comatose. Ventilated and frail, he underwent a bone marrow biopsy. The result: multiple myeloma, an aggressive bone cancer. His son erupted. "He walked in here! You did this!"

Denial curdled into rage. He withheld payment, sued the hospital, and dragged us to consumer court. Although we won, the scars lingered. My neurologist colleague muttered, "We diagnosed a zebra in 72 hours. Now we're villains?"

Such cases birth a corrosive dilemma. As a tertiary center, we attract dire, complex cases—precisely those most vulnerable to tragic outcomes. Defensive medicine whispers: Turn them away. Play it safe. But then who'd treat the woman with the undiagnosed autoimmune storm? The child with a mystery fever? An acute coronary syndrome with cardiogenic shock? We walk a knife's edge—protecting lives while shielding ourselves from blame.

The son's lawsuit, though baseless, exposed a rot in the system: distrust weaponized by ignorance or opportunism. Medical indemnity insurance shields our finances, not our morale. Each frivolous case erodes camaraderie, making junior doctors wary of cardiology, oncology or neurosurgery. The collateral damage? Patients themselves. When skepticism poisons the well, the best healers flee.

Yet I return to Mrs. Hameeda's biryani. To the farmer's okra, still dusty from his fields. For every family that brandishes a lawyer's card, a dozen more clasp our hands in silent thanks. Trust isn't naivety—it's a pact. We pledge competence; patients grant us the grace to be human.

Some will always see malice in misfortune, but most? Most still believe.

And so, we keep fighting—for them.

*****

During a monthly clinical governance meeting, Mr. Anand highlighted the concerning rise in patient complaints and litigations. Dr. Raj Kiran, Dr. Mohan, Shabnam, and I proposed actionable solutions. To ensure objectivity, we conducted surveys and performed a retrospective analysis of patient feedback. The following measures were adopted:

1. Transparency as the Cornerstone

    -   Open Communication: Physicians must clearly explain the patient's condition, disease severity, prognosis, treatment plan, and estimated hospitalization costs.
    -   Family Engagement: Regular counseling sessions and family meetings to align expectations and address concerns.
    -   Role of Medical Social Workers: Act as liaisons to bridge gaps in understanding between patients and healthcare providers.

2. Financial Clarity

    -   Cost Transparency: Billing executives provide real-time, itemized cost estimates to prevent financial surprises.
    -   For patients facing financial constraints, crowdfunding through private organizations can be facilitated as a viable support option.

3. Proactive Feedback Mechanisms

    -   Continuous Feedback: Caregivers can submit grievances during hospitalization and at discharge via structured feedback forms.
    -   Mortality Reviews: Monthly audits of all deaths to identify systemic gaps and implement preventive strategies.
    -   Complaint Resolution: Major complaints are analyzed in clinical review meetings to refine protocols and staff training.

What was the Impact?

These interventions significantly boosted patient and caregiver satisfaction, reduced negative feedback by 40%, and curtailed litigations.

Trust, we realized, thrives when transparency meets empathy.

10

CHAPTER 10

*They say a person needs just three
things to be happy in this world:
someone to love, something to do,
and something to hope for.*

–Tom Bodett

The year 2008 unfurled like a sunlit tapestry, each thread woven with milestones that shimmered with promise and joy. At its heart was Muskan, whose recent triumph in completing her postgraduate course in Obstetrics and Gynecology stood as a testament to her relentless dedication. Her thesis, "*Maternal Health in Rural Landscapes: Bridging Gaps Through Community Care,*" had not only earned accolades but also sparked discussions at national conferences—a feat that left me awestruck. I'd never glimpsed this scholarly facet of her; she'd never mentioned her research ambitions, nor hinted at the depth of her intellect. To me, she remained the same effervescent soul who lit up rooms with her laughter, forever poised to playfully rib anyone within earshot.

The winds of change swept in swiftly for Muskan. Mere months after donning her postgraduate cap, she found herself betrothed to Azeem, a charming young man. Their engagement unfolded as a whirlwind affair in Vizag, where the Bay of Bengal's turquoise waves witnessed a ceremony steeped in elegance—one we couldn't attend due to prior work obligations.

Azeem, her fiancé, was a revelation. As Managing Director of Star Pharmaceuticals, a venture his father had founded after decades in public health, he carried the weight of legacy with unassuming grace. The company, though young, had already carved a niche by producing generics for diseases like diabetes and hypertension—medicines priced not for profit but for accessibility. Last monsoon, Star had partnered with rural clinics to distribute free antimalarial kits, a project Azeem spearheaded after visiting a village where children played barefoot in mosquito-riddled puddles. Muskan often recounted how he'd rejected a lucrative buyout offer from a multinational conglomerate. "They wanted to hike prices by 200%," he'd told her, his usually calm voice sharpening. "I'd rather dissolve the company than betray our mission." This unyielding integrity, paired with a work ethic, made him a figure of quiet admiration. Despite their wealth, Muskaan described his family as down-to-earth.

One weekend, Muskaan insisted on introducing Azeem to Shabnam and me, still mock-scowling over our absence at her engagement. "You two owe me years of explanations!" she'd grumbled earlier, though her indignation—true to her nature—dissolved into giggles by sunset. When Azeem flew to Hyderabad for a conference, she orchestrated a reunion dinner at a waterside restaurant, her enthusiasm undimmed by our prior lapse.

Azeem cut an impressive figure in his navy blazer, his calm demeanor a counterpoint to Muskaan's electric energy. She bounced between our table and the buffet, her crimson saree fluttering like a banner of joy, until Shabnam finally tugged her into a chair.

"I'm still furious with both of you," Muskaan declared, jabbing her fork theatrically at us. "But how could I not show off my prized acquisition?"

Shabnam raised her palms in surrender. "Guilty as charged—we're at your mercy."

Muskaan's grin widened. "Rehan, your loss is Azeem's gain. Shabnam, meet my fiancé!" She flung an arm toward Azeem, nearly upending her mango lassi.

"An excellent choice," Shabnam replied, her eyes crinkling.

"That's why I rushed the engagement—before he could have second thoughts," Muskaan quipped, winking at me. I sensed the playful jab was meant for me.

I chuckled, recognizing the barb meant to nudge old memories. "We're thrilled to finally meet," I said, turning to Azeem. "You've clearly found someone extraordinary."

"The pleasure is mine. Yes, Muskaan is amazing," he replied, smiling.

"Azeem, how's the pharmaceutical industry faring these days?" I inquired, leaning forward with genuine curiosity.

"Sir, it's a vast field with numerous players. Success depends on your goals, vision, and mission," he replied, steepling his fingers thoughtfully.

"Isn't it mostly about profit-making?" I asked continuing the conversation.

Azeem's gaze sharpened, his voice steady with conviction. "Perhaps for most, but not for us. Dr. Rehan, we focus on providing quality medicine at affordable prices." His candidness was refreshing; he seemed genuinely committed to his work.

"Boys will be boys; they only talk work," Muskaan interjected playfully.

Indeed, we had been engrossed in our discussion, momentarily overlooking the delightful company of the two ladies. Afterwards, our conversation shifted to lighter topics like cuisine, fashion, and films. It was a pleasant evening that ended all too soon.

The wedding unfolded like a Bollywood spectacle at Hyderabad's Falak Numa Palace, its marble courtyards draped in jasmine garlands and twinkling fairy lights. Imran and Suhana, my ever-efficient brother and sister-in-law, had orchestrated every detail—from the fragrant biryani stations to the qawwali singers whose voices soared beneath the stars. Suhana, her silk saree shimmering like moonlight, corralled tardy relatives with the precision of a general, while Imran negotiated with florists in fluent Telugu.

Toward the end of the wedding reception, I found Muskaan by the rose-strewn exit gate, her gold-embroidered lehenga catching the lantern light as she bade farewell to guests. She turned, her smile widening—a reflex as natural as breathing.

"True to your name," I said, clasping her hands, "you must always wear this smile, Muskaan. Seeing you this radiant… it lifts a mountain of guilt from my chest."

She laughed, the sound bright as temple bells. "Oh, Rehan, don't you know? Matches are stitched in heaven. You and Shabnam… Azeem and me—" Her gaze drifted to where her husband stood, laughing with a circle of cousins. "We've all found our missing pieces."

Shortly thereafter, Muskaan relocated to Visakhapatnam (Vizag) to settle with her in-laws and commence her clinical practice, embarking on this new chapter with the quiet determination that had always defined her.

******

My medical practice at Hope Ray flourished, anchored by the trust I had earned from senior colleagues and the respect I commanded from peers and junior staff alike. Esteemed specialists like Dr. Raj Kiran, our cardiologist, and Dr. Mohan Varma, the neurologist, frequently sought my counsel—a testament to the professional credibility I'd cultivated. Beyond patient care, I remained deeply invested in mentoring residents and nursing teams, fostering an environment of collaborative learning. My consistent collaboration with the executive team further solidified my reputation as a unifying force between clinical and administrative spheres. This multifaceted engagement brought me to the attention of senior leadership, who began to view me as more than a physician—a strategic asset.

One afternoon, an unexpected summons arrived from the CEO's office.

"Dr. Rehan," he began, gesturing to the chair opposite his mahogany desk, "your clinical excellence is undisputed, but it's your leadership ethos that intrigues us. We're seeking a Medical Director who embodies not only expertise, but uncompromising integrity. The role would allow you to retain your practice while shaping institutional protocols. With the board's full support, would you consider steering this vision?"

The proposal hung in the air—an uncharted frontier demanding equal parts pragmatism and idealism. Yet hesitation never surfaced; challenges of this magnitude were why I'd entered medicine.

"Your confidence humbles me, sir," I replied, leaning forward. "I accept this responsibility with the understanding that my first duty remains to our patients. You have my word: I will bridge clinical and administrative priorities without compromising either."

That evening, I returned home as dusk painted the sky in amber streaks, my heart thrumming with the day's revelation. Shabnam sat by the balcony, her silhouette framed against the fading light, a half-finished embroidery hoop abandoned beside her. The familiar scent of cardamom chai lingered in the air as she handed me a steaming cup, her eyes crinkling at the edges in silent welcome.

"Shabnam," I began, tracing the rim of my teacup, "I've… something to share."

Her laughter danced like wind chimes. "What synchronicity! I, too, have news. But you first," she insisted, tucking a loose strand of hair behind her ear—a gesture I'd come to recognize as her quiet way of masking anticipation.

I leaned forward, the words tumbling out before I could temper them. "The CEO offered me the Medical Director position today."

Her teacup clinked against the saucer as she set it down. "Oh, Rehan! This is wonderful" she exclaimed, clasping my hands. "Good things don't go unnoticed. If there's anyone more suited for the role, it's you."

A wave of relief washed over me as she nodded—her silent endorsement more affirming than any accolade. But her earlier words now buzzed in my mind like unquiet bees.

"Your turn," I prompted, studying the blush creeping up her neck.

Shabnam hesitated, her gaze dropping to her lap. When she finally looked up, her eyes glistened with a secret joy I hadn't seen since our wedding day. "It's… our news," she whispered, guiding my palm to rest gently below her navel.

"I am pregnant!" she added, her voice trembling with awe and disbelief.

I pulled her into a joyous embrace, my cheek pressed against her hair, breathing in the jasmine oil she'd worn since our courting days.

"A director and a father," I murmured into her crown. "Allah's blessings wear disguises, don't they?"

She laughed—a sound now laced with tears—and nestled deeper into my arms. Outside, the first stars blinked awake, bearing witness to a twilight where two futures unfurled as one.

CHAPTER 11

*We fight, even against insurmountable
odds, because sometimes we win.*

–Billy Parish

Shabnam continued her work at Hope Ray late into her pregnancy. Even as her belly swelled with the promise of new life, she refused to relinquish her post, insisting that tending to her patients grounded her. Her pregnancy unfolded without complication: blood pressure steady, scans pristine, every antenatal checkup affirming her robust health.

Dr. Vimala, our obstetrician—a woman whose calm demeanor belied her razor-sharp expertise—became our guiding star. With the patience of a storyteller and the precision of a scientist, she would meticulously decode Shabnam's progress for us, her hands moving with practiced grace during examinations.

"Your wife," she'd say, her eyes crinkling behind wire-framed glasses, "is as resilient as they come. This little one's already learning from the best."

When our baby's arrival finally dawned, it felt less like a medical event and more like a quiet cosmic alignment. Shabnam's labor, much like her pregnancy, defied drama. There were no frantic dashes or panicked shouts. Only the steady rhythm of her breath, the reassuring hum of monitors, and Dr. Vimala's murmured encouragements. By sunrise, our daughter slipped into the world with a cry that sounded oddly like a sigh of relief, as though she, too, had been waiting to meet us.

Inara, the name my father tenderly proposed for our newborn daughter, carried an ethereal weight. Derived from its ancient roots meaning "heaven-sent," it felt like a divine whisper, symbolizing not just a beacon of light but a promise of hope. The moment he shared it, the name struck a universal chord, weaving itself seamlessly into our family's story. After gentle deliberation, it was unanimously chosen, as though destiny itself had etched it into her identity.

Inara's birth unfolded as a radiant blessing, casting warmth over every corner of our lives. My parents, their eyes glistening with tears, overflowed with delight at the arrival of their first granddaughter, cradling her as though she were spun from stardust. For me, her presence became an anchor. After grueling days spent in the sterile glow of hospital corridors, stepping through the front door to see Inara's serene face—framed by wisps of downy hair and eyes like twin constellations—became my most cherished ritual. One glance at her delicate features, and the weariness would melt away, replaced by a surge of vitality. She was a living sonnet, a quiet revolution of joy that recalibrated my soul. Inara's arrival had truly illuminated our lives, stitching the ordinary with threads of the extraordinary.

Two weeks later, the fragile calm shattered.

My phone buzzed violently in my pocket. It was a call from my mother. Her voice, usually steady, trembled like a frayed wire.

"Rehan, something's wrong with Shabnam. She's… not herself. Her words are slurring, her eyes—they're vacant. Please, come home. Now." The plea in her tone clawed at my chest.

I abandoned everything, my car tires screeching against asphalt as I tore through traffic, my mind a storm of fragmented fears. The drive blurred into a nightmare. Medical jargon—hypoxia, cerebral edema, postpartum eclampsia—pulsed like a siren in my head. I gripped the steering wheel until my knuckles whitened, praying the almighty God. Then, my phone rang again. This time, my mother's scream pierced the silence: "She's seizing, Rehan! Her whole body—it's jerking, she's not breathing—!"

"Turn her onto her side!" I barked, my voice raw. "I'm calling an ambulance!" My fingers fumbled over the phone, dialing 100 with a numb, mechanical urgency.

I arrived to chaos.

The ambulance's rotating lights bathed our street in lurid reds and blues, casting long, frantic shadows. Paramedics crouched over Shabnam's limp form on the living room floor, her skin pallid and clammy, her chest rising in shallow, uneven hitches. Postictal state, I registered numbly—the hollow aftermath of a storm. Her eyelids fluttered, but recognition didn't return. My mother stood frozen in the corner, her face streaked with tears, clutching Inara's swaddle to her chest like a talisman.

"We're transporting her to Hope Ray. Now," a paramedic snapped, strapping Shabnam to a gurney. I climbed into the ambulance, my hand clasping hers—cold, unresponsive. The sirens wailed as we sped through intersections, time dilating into a sickening haze. Each second stretched into an eternity, every breath she took a fragile victory.

Hope Ray's ER loomed ahead, its fluorescent lights a harsh, impersonal glare. Nurses swarmed Shabnam; their voices sharp with protocol. I hovered in the doorway, my shirt stained with sweat and dread, whispering promises to a universe that felt suddenly, cruelly indifferent.

Dr. Mohan Varma, our neurologist and a man whose reputation for swift, unflinching diagnoses preceded him, swung into action the moment Shabnam arrived. His hands moved with the precision of a chess master as he conducted a rapid neurological exam: pupils reactive, reflexes intact, but her speech slurred and fragmented.

"We need imaging now," he ordered, his voice clipped yet calm.

The MRI machine hummed ominously as Shabnam lay motionless inside, its magnetic waves mapping the labyrinth of her brain. When the results flashed onto the screen, Dr. Mohan's brow furrowed. He gestured me closer, his finger tapping a hazy shadow on the parietal lobe.

"Dr. Rehan, this is… perplexing," he confessed, uncharacteristically hesitant. "There's a minor hemorrhage here—a smudge of bleed on the scan—but no trauma, no vascular malformations. The why eludes us."

He leaned back, steepling his fingers. "Postpartum cortical venous sinus thrombosis is my leading suspicion. The timing fits—a clot forming in the dural sinuses after delivery—but the radiologist can't pinpoint the occlusion site." He pulled up the angiogram, tracing the serpentine veins. "See here? The transverse sinus appears narrowed, suggestive of thrombosis…??? but without the definitive 'empty delta' sign or clear filling defects. It's like chasing a ghost."

A cold dread seeped into my bones. I knew the stakes: untreated CVST could spiral into cerebral edema, recurrent seizures, worse. Yet the ambiguity paralyzed us—how do you wage war on an enemy you can't fully see? I absorbed the deluge of information, my mind racing to reconcile logic with dread. The paradox hung like a blade: act without certainty, or wait and risk catastrophe.

"If we administer anticoagulants blindly," I said, forcing my voice to steady, "we risk aggravating the hemorrhage. But withholding treatment could allow a silent clot to spread further. How do we navigate this… gray zone?"

Dr. Mohan met my gaze, his expression a mosaic of professional resolve and quiet empathy.

"You've distilled the dilemma perfectly, Rehan," he replied, his tone measured yet heavy. "Without a definitive diagnosis, we're balancing on a knife's edge. One misstep in either direction…" He paused, the unspoken consequences thickening the air.

I clenched my jaw, frustration and fear knotting in my chest. "Then what's our move? Do we gamble? Wait for clearer signs?"

He hesitated, a rare crack in his usual decisiveness. "Our radiologist here is competent, but…" He leaned forward, lowering his voice as if sharing a classified truth. "He's not infallible. Two years ago, we had Dr. Vikas—a savant with a gift for decoding even the most ambiguous scans. Rehan, his eye is unparalleled."

A flicker of hope. "You're suggesting we consult him?"

"Immediately," Dr. Mohan urged, scribbling a number on a slip of paper. "If anyone can pinpoint the occlusion or rule it out, it's Vikas. Time isn't our ally, but neither is recklessness."

Dr. Vikas—sharp-eyed, relentlessly curious, and a man whose reputation for brilliance had only grown since his abrupt exit from Hope Ray—was no stranger to me. We'd crossed paths years ago, when his restless intellect and penchant for challenging institutional complacency had made him both admired and quietly resented. His departure had been abrupt, whispered about in hospital corridors as a clash of philosophies. Yet here he was, now the founder of Lumia Diagnostics, a boutique imaging center whose glass-and-steel facade gleamed like a fortress of sleek monitors and unorthodox diagnoses.

He greeted me not with small talk, but a firm handshake and laser focus, his gaze already darting to the scans tucked under my arm. I'd briefed him earlier—Shabnam's sudden collapse, the ambiguous hemorrhage, the paralyzing uncertainty—but now, in person, his intensity sharpened.

"Let's not waste time," he said, ushering me into a dimly lit room where a bank of high-resolution screens cast an eerie blue glow.

The silence as he reviewed the images was nerve-shredding. His fingers danced across the keyboard, zooming, rotating, layering angiograms over MRIs with the precision of a conductor. Finally, he leaned back, tapping a slender pointer at a shadowy curve on the screen. "Here's the crux," he said, voice steady. "Many mistake a hypoplastic left transverse sinus—a congenital narrowness—for thrombosis on MR venography. It's a common pitfall." He zoomed in, revealing the vein's delicate, unbroken thread. "This isn't your culprit. The bleed's origin lies here."

My breath hitched as he highlighted a hairline occlusion in a tiny parietal cortical vein, its rupture barely visible. "Pressure built up here," he explained, "causing a localized bleed. The seizure was likely a downstream effect—irritation of the adjacent cortex."

"Anticoagulants?" I pressed, the weight of dread and hope warring in my chest.

"Absolutely." His tone brooked no doubt. "The bleed is contained, but the clot? If it propagates…" He let the implication hang, then met my eyes. "The risk of re-bleed is negligible compared to the catastrophic cascade you'd face without thinners. Start heparin. Now."

Relief and terror coiled together as I stood. In his certainty, I found not just answers, but a lifeline—one forged by a mind that saw clarity where others saw shadows. Stunned by the precision of his analysis, I clasped his hand, my voice thick with gratitude. "Thank you, Doctor. You've given us more than answers—you've given us a path."

He waved off the praise with a humble shrug, though pride flickered in his eyes. "It's my privilege, Dr. Rehan. Medicine is a team sport, isn't it?"

The question lingered on my tongue, unprofessional yet irresistible. "Forgive my curiosity," I ventured, "but why leave Hope Ray? You were…incomparable there."

He responded candidly, "I sought a broader range of diagnostic challenges. The patient demographic at Hope Ray was quite specific. Here, I can serve a diverse clientele at affordable rates. Additionally, my freelance work with other diagnostic centers keeps me professionally fulfilled."

I nodded, struck by his idealism. "Inshallah, our paths cross again. The field needs more like you."

Back at Hope Ray, I hurried to Dr. Mohan's office, clutching Dr. Vikas's report like a sacred manuscript. The neurologist listened intently as I detailed the findings, his stern expression softening into a nod of respect. "A cortical vein occlusion…" he murmured, stroking his chin. "Vikas always did see what others missed."

Shabnam's recovery unfolded like a slow sunrise. The heparin worked its quiet magic, her lucidity returning in fragments—first a flicker of recognition in her eyes, then her voice, raspy but unmistakably hers, teasing me for forgetting her favorite tea. By discharge day, she sat upright in bed, Inara cradled in her arms, her smile brighter than the sunlight streaming through the window.

I sank into the chair beside her, the weight of the ordeal crashing over me.

"We're doctors," I said, my voice frayed with exhaustion. "We know the system, the jargon, the shortcuts—and still, it took a labyrinth of misreads, second opinions, and sheer luck to save you. What chance does someone without our privilege have?"

She turned to me, her gaze steady, "You fought for me, Rehan. That's the lesson here. Not the hurdles, but the refusal to let them win." Her hand brushed mine, warm and sure. "The real test isn't just knowing the right path. It's convincing others to walk it with you."

I thought of Dr. Vikas's dimly lit lab, Dr. Mohan's grudging admiration, the ambulance crew's split-second choices. "And walking it yourself," I added quietly, "even when every sign screams to turn back."

Inara stirred in her arms, a soft whimper breaking the silence. Shabnam laughed—a sound I'd feared I'd never hear again—and pressed a kiss to our daughter's forehead. "Look at her," she whispered. "Our reminder that some battles are worth every step."

12

CHAPTER 12

Let the beauty of what you love be what you do.

–Rumi

In 2009, a few years after assuming the role of Medical Director at the hospital, my days unfolded in a whirlwind of responsibilities. Balancing my dual obligations as a practicing physician and an administrative leader, I navigated the delicate equilibrium between direct patient care and the strategic oversight of hospital operations. Our institution thrived under a meticulously coordinated system, a testament to the seamless partnership I shared with Mr. Anand, our seasoned hospital administrator. Through our collaborative efforts, we cultivated a culture of patient-centered care, embedding principles of quality, safety, and compassion into every protocol and practice.

One morning, as dawn's first light crept through my window, the shrill ring of my phone pierced the quiet. On the line was Dr. Padmavati, our esteemed senior gynecologist, her voice taut with worry.

"Dr. Rehan, I'm terribly sorry to disturb you at this hour," she began, her tone uncharacteristically hesitant. "But I need your expertise. My daughter has been unwell for two days—persistent fever, coughing, and shortness of breath. I fear it may be a severe respiratory infection."

Though still groggy, I straightened instinctively, my clinical instincts overriding the early hour. "Please, there's no need to apologize," I assured her, slipping into the calm, measured cadence I reserved for anxious families. "Bring her to the Emergency Room immediately. I'll meet you there within the hour to assess her myself."

Upon examining Lalitha, a 22-year-old woman presenting with a three-day history of fever, productive cough, and intermittent diarrhea, I noted her visibly distressed state. She appeared febrile, her skin flushed and damp with perspiration, while her labored breathing suggested underlying respiratory compromise. A pulse oximeter reading confirmed mild hypoxemia at 92% saturation, and subsequent chest radiography revealed bilateral patchy infiltrates. These were hallmarks of developing pneumonia. Recognizing the urgency, I ordered her immediate admission to the Medical Intensive Care Unit (MICU) for oxygen therapy and continuous monitoring. Turning to Shabnam, I emphasized the need for hourly vital sign assessments and strict adherence to the sepsis protocol. "Alert me of any decline in her oxygen levels or mentation," I instructed, before gently reassuring Dr. Padmavati, "We're prioritizing her stabilization. She's in capable hands here."

Dr. Padmavati lingered, her clinical composure fraying as she clasped her trembling hands. "There's... something else," she confessed, her voice thinning. "Lalitha was engaged just five days ago. The wedding is in four weeks. Her fiancé's family..." She trailed off, the unspoken weight of societal expectations hanging between us.

Meeting her gaze, I tempered professionalism with empathy. "I cannot promise timelines, but I can promise vigilance," I said firmly. "Every decision we make—from antibiotics to fluid management—will be guided by one goal: restoring her health without compromise."

After Lalitha's transfer to the Medical Intensive Care Unit, Shabnam and the critical care team swiftly initiated broad-spectrum antibiotics and hemodynamic monitoring. Yet, despite aggressive intervention, her respiratory distress deepened within hours, her oxygen saturation plummeting to 88% on room air. Alarms blared as she struggled against the encroaching hypoxia, necessitating urgent escalation to high-flow nasal cannula support. I sprinted to the MICU, my shoes clicking sharply against the linoleum, arriving to find Lalitha gasping, her fingertips tinged with cyanosis.

Her eyes locked onto mine, wide with terror, as she forced the words through ragged breaths: "Doctor… will I… survive this?"

I leaned closer, steadying my voice against the cacophony of monitors. "You will," I affirmed, squeezing her clammy hand. "Focus on breathing. And when this passes, your wedding will be all the sweeter for the fight you're winning today."

Her grip tightened momentarily. "My fiancé… in Pune…" she wheezed, tears mingling with sweat on her temples. "He's had fever… cough… since yesterday. Should he—?"

"Shhh, conserve your strength," I interjected softly, adjusting her oxygen to 15L/min. "We'll stabilize you first. But yes—he must contact a Pune hospital immediately. These symptoms demand urgency."

As I stepped out of the MICU, a chilling realization dawned: Pune, where Lalitha's fiancé resided, had recently emerged as an epicenter of Influenza A H1N1. This was a virulent strain notorious for triggering fatal pneumonia in young, otherwise healthy adults. My stomach tightened. Two patients, one city, the same timeline. I whispered a silent plea for Lalitha and her fiancé to defy the virus's grim statistics.

Without delay, I inquired about the testing process and the antiviral medication, Oseltamivir. We faced significant challenges in acquiring the Nasopharyngeal swab kit, but eventually sent it to the Institute of Preventive Medicine in Narayanaguda, expecting the report the following day. Oseltamivir was not readily available either, as it was classified under Schedule X drugs by the government to prevent misuse. Nevertheless, by evening, we managed to obtain the medication and commenced Lalitha's empirical treatment.

Dawn brought no reprieve. Lalitha's lungs rebelled—oxygen saturation nosedived to 82%, her chest X-ray now streaked with the ground-glass opacities of early ARDS. When the H1N1 result flashed positive, the unit erupted into controlled chaos. Swine flu. Our first confirmed case. No isolation protocols. No trained staff. Only instinct. I called an emergency huddle, mandating masks, contact gowns, and prophylactic Tamiflu for every exposed team member. "Assume airborne transmission," I warned. "One misstep, and this unit becomes an outbreak zone

Dr. Padmavati was understandably tense during this period, deeply concerned about Lalitha's response to the treatment. Shabnam provided regular updates, maintaining a glimmer of hope— "Her fever's dipping," "Kidney function stable"—while I charted the agonizing wait for the antivirals to claw back ground.

Seventy-two hours later, Lalitha's X-ray cleared like storm clouds parting. We weaned her off the ventilator in increments, her voice returning in a hoarse whisper: "Thank you." When she gripped her mother's hand unaided, the unit exhaled as one—a chorus of muffled cheers behind masks.

Lalitha was discharged five days later. On the morning of her release, she stood in the sunlit hospital corridor, clutching my hands in hers. Her eyes glistened with unshed tears, the weight of gratitude and resilience mingling in her gaze.

"Doctor," she began, her voice trembling slightly, "I don't know if this ordeal was a test from God… but I do know you were my guardian angel." She paused, tightening her grip as if anchoring herself to the moment. "No words can ever thank you enough, but I won't take 'no' for an answer. You and Dr. Shabnam must attend my wedding."

I smiled warmly, touched by her resolve. "We wouldn't miss it," I replied. "Save us front-row seats. We'll be there to see you shine in your bridal finery."

True to our word, we attended her wedding a month later. Lalitha stood resplendent in a silk sari embroidered with gold, her smile eclipsing the jewels adorning her. Amid the joyous clamor of drums and laughter, she guided her groom toward us. "These two," she declared, her voice steady and proud, "gave me back my future. Today, I promise to honor that gift."

We pressed blessings into their palms—a ritual as old as tradition itself—and stepped back, humbled by the weight of our calling. In that moment, the clatter of hospital monitors faded, replaced by the rhythm of a new beginning. This, I thought, is why we fight.

Following Lalitha's case, we convened an emergency multidisciplinary task force comprising physicians, ENT specialists, pulmonologists, nursing heads, and hospital executives. Our objectives were threefold: to develop a coordinated screening strategy, implement rigorous isolation protocols, and standardize antiviral treatment guidelines for H1N1 influenza. Over the ensuing months, we treated and successfully discharged hundreds of Swine flu patients, though tragically, several succumbed to the infection despite our vigilance. In every instance, however, our teams fought relentlessly to deliver evidence-based, compassionate care.

By May 2010, India's official H1N1 case count had surpassed 10,000—a figure representing only the documented tip of a far larger iceberg, as countless mild cases went untested and unreported. The confirmed death toll exceeded 1,000, a grim testament to the virus's capacity to mutate from a seasonal nuisance into a lethal global threat. To this day, it remains staggering how swiftly a seemingly benign pathogen can evolve into an agent of chaos. Whether humanity will face similar pandemics in the coming decades remains unknown. But history offers one certainty: without sustained investment in surveillance, infrastructure, and public health preparedness, we risk repeating the same devastating cycle—and the price of complacency will always be measured in lives.

13

CHAPTER 13

*Learning and innovation go hand in hand.
The arrogance of success is to think that
what you did yesterday will be
sufficient for tomorrow.*

–William Pollard

Then there were years of progress.

A few years passed, and Shabnam and I were immersed in our work. The patient care was so exemplary that it seemed nothing could go wrong. With the lowest mortality rates, I became known as the doctor whose patients didn't die. Though in truth, it was Shabnam who refused to let them succumb. Her Critical Care Unit performed extraordinarily, earning widespread acclaim from all quarters.

One afternoon, as sunlight slanted across the cluttered desk of my office, a space typically reserved for clinical paperwork and administrative labyrinths, Shabnam appeared in my office doorway. It was an unusual sight, given our routines rarely intersected outside the ICU.

"To what do I owe this honor?" I teased, gesturing to the chair across from me. "How can I help?" I asked, setting aside a stack of discharge summaries.

She stepped inside, her usual calm edged with restless energy.

"Rehan," she began, perching on the edge of a chair, "I've been mapping out an idea. One that could reshape how we handle critical referrals."

I leaned forward. "I'm all ears."

"Every week, we receive dozens of terminal cases from peripheral centers—patients so deteriorated that even our best efforts feel like racing against time. But what if we intercept them earlier?" Her words quickened. "Imagine a hub where we guide smaller hospitals in real time. Stabilize patients before they crash into our ER."

"As a tertiary center, we're already drowning in complex cases," I countered, though intrigued. "How would this differ?"

"By creating a Critical Care Command Center," she said, her eyes alight. "A 24/7 digital bridge between our ICU and their staff. They'd share live patient data—histories, imaging, labs—while we advise on interventions and triage. No more guessing games. No more delays."

The vision crystallized: a neural network of care, pulsating with shared expertise. "You're proposing we become their lifeline," I murmured.

"Exactly. We'd reduce mortality and streamline referrals." She pulled up a mock interface on her tablet—dashboards glowing with vitals, chat threads buzzing with consults. "Outcomes would speak for themselves."

A laugh of sheer possibility escaped me. "This isn't just good. It's revolutionary. Let's take it to the CEO."

One month later, the Critical Care Command Center was launched under Shabnam's meticulous direction. Monitors lined the walls like sentinels, alive with data streams from a dozen clinics. By week two, stabilized patients began arriving with coherent charts and controlled symptoms—a stark contrast to the chaos we'd once normalized. Referrals tripled, yet our ICU's efficiency improved, survival rates climbing by 18%. Hope Ray's reputation soared as a beacon of innovation.

At a staff celebration, Shabnam stood quietly in the corner, observing the hum of her creation. I joined her, nodding toward a screen where a nurse in remote nursing home was administering a lifesaving vasopressor under our guidance.

"You've rewritten the rules," I said.

She smiled. "We did."

Collaborating with colleagues across specialties, I sought to pioneer innovative programs that would distinguish our hospital clinically. I proposed establishing dedicated clinics for tuberculosis (TB), HIV, and lifestyle-related conditions such as obesity management and smoking cessation. Meanwhile, Dr. Raj Kiran spearheaded the creation of specialized units for heart failure, pacemaker management, and arrhythmia care. Departmental meetings buzzed with discussions of additional focused clinics—pain management, epilepsy, menopause support, and more—each designed to address unmet patient needs. We meticulously outlined infrastructure upgrades, resource allocations, and staffing requirements for these initiatives. Progress was steady, each step fortifying our reputation as a leader in patient-centered innovation.

*****

One Sunday, while attending a diabetes conference, I unexpectedly crossed paths with Dr. Rakesh Kumar, a senior colleague from my medical school days. His eyes widened in a mix of delight and disbelief as he approached me.

"Rehan!" he exclaimed, clasping my shoulder. "I never imagined corporate physicians like you would spare time for academic pursuits. This is a welcome surprise."

"Dr. Rakesh, it's good to see you," I replied, sidestepping the subtle jab. His words pricked at an old wound—the unspoken divide between corporate practitioners and academia. Most of us in private hospitals, I knew, rarely engaged in teaching, a truth that had always gnawed at me.

He tilted his head, his tone softening with paternal pride. "We government doctors may not match your salaries, but teaching medical students, molding future healers, gives us a joy no paycheck can rival."

The remark lingered in my mind long after we parted.

That evening, I found Shabnam reviewing a patient report in our sunlit living room.

"Rakesh made me realize something today," I confessed, staring at the steam curling from my chai. "I've built a career, but not a legacy."

She set down her pen, studying me with that quiet intensity that always preceded her breakthroughs. After a weighted pause, she leaned forward, her eyes alight. "Why assume you can't teach, Rehan? You'd excel as a mentor. And you wouldn't need to abandon Hope Ray."

I frowned. "Without academia's infrastructure, how?"

"The DNB program," she countered, as if the answer had always been obvious. "If we tailor our hospital to meet its accreditation standards, we could host postgraduate residencies ourselves. Imagine—students learning from your protocols, your innovations!"

The idea struck like a defibrillator's jolt. Within months, we'd submitted applications for DNB accreditation in Medicine, Cardiology, Neurology, and Nephrology. When the approval letter arrived, I traced the embossed seal with trembling fingers. Hope Ray wasn't just a hospital now—it was a beacon for the next generation of doctors.

That night, as Shabnam and I celebrated with Gulab Jamun shared straight from the box, I finally understood Rakesh's quiet pride. Legacy, I realized, isn't forged in titles or institutions, but in the minds you ignite and the futures you shape.

*****

During a quarterly strategy meeting, the air thick with the scent of freshly printed reports and simmering coffee, I presented a proposal that would redefine our hospital's legacy.

"Colleagues," I began, tapping the NABH accreditation brochure against the conference table, "this isn't just a certification—it's a covenant with our patients."

Mr. Anand, our pragmatic administrator, leaned back in his leather chair. "What tangible benefits would this bring, Dr. Rehan? Metrics matter more than plaques on walls."

"NABH accreditation," I explained, projecting a slide of its gold-and-blue emblem, "is a globally recognized seal auditing everything from infection control protocols to ethical governance. It tells families we don't just meet standards—we set them."

His pen hovered over a cost analysis sheet. "Hmm... It would distinguish us in this corporate hospital arms race."

"Precisely. Patients increasingly choose institutions prioritizing transparency and safety over glossy brochures."

"But the financial bleed?" he pressed. "Structural upgrades... training man-hours..."

"An investment, not an expense," I countered. "Imagine the ROI when we become the city's first NABH-accredited facility. The trust it builds, the partnerships it unlocks."

Six Months Later.

The accreditation process unfolded like a military campaign. We reforged protocols: nurses rehearsed emergency drills under stopwatches, architects reworked wards to millimeter-precise safety margins, and our janitorial staff became unsung heroes mastering biohazard disposal. When the NABH auditors arrived—clipboards in hand, questions sharper than scalpels—we stood ready.

Their final report read like a love letter to excellence.

At the celebration gala, fairy lights twined around the NABH plaque as the CEO toasted with sparkling pomegranate juice. "To Dr. Rehan's vision," he declared, "and to every hand that turned policy into practice!"

I found Mr. Anand by the dessert cart, uncharacteristically sentimental. "You were right," he admitted, gesturing at the crowd of beaming staff. "This… pride in their work—it's priceless."

14

CHAPTER 14

*Health is a state of complete physical,
mental and social well-being and not
merely the absence of disease or infirmity.*

–World Health Organization

The bright lights of Hope Ray Hospital flashed relentlessly, casting a sterile glow over the bustling corridors. Here, the rhythm of life was dictated by beeping monitors and hurried footsteps. For healthcare providers, the unspoken rule was clear: keep moving, no matter the cost. Dr. Wilson often joked that the hospital's motto should be "We save lives, but forget to live ours." The irony was bitter. Nurses juggled double shifts, residents survived on caffeine, and senior cardiologist like Dr. Raj Kiran wore their exhaustion like a badge of honor. Denial wasn't just a coping mechanism; it was a survival tactic.

While some destressed through avocations such as music, golf, poetry, or vacations, most absorbed the pressure and carried on as if nothing had happened. The social lives of doctors are often pitiable. They rarely meet relatives or friends, interacting primarily with patients and colleagues. Even on the rare occasion they attend a social gathering, they are seldom spared. Relatives seize the opportunity to consult them about medical issues mid-conversation. You feel frustrated but cannot protest. After all, you're expected to remain humble and courteous.

This chronic stress takes a gradual but relentless toll.

We had a young, dynamic surgeon in his thirties, Dr. Prathap. A nonsmoker and teetotaler, he spent most of his time at the hospital and was the management's blue-eyed boy, performing the highest number of surgeries with excellent outcomes.

One morning, Dr. Prathap arrived at the ER with chest discomfort. He'd had a late dinner the previous night and assumed it was indigestion. Shockingly, it turned out to be a heart attack.

"Dr. Rehan, I have no risk factors. How could this happen?" he asked, stunned.

I was at a loss for words. If this could happen to someone like him, how were any of us safe?

"Dr. Prathap, let's focus on treating you first. Then we'll investigate the cause," said Dr. Raj Kiran, preparing for the coronary intervention.

After the procedure, Dr. Prathap stabilized. I met Dr. Raj Kiran and asked,

"What caused this? Were there significant coronary blockages?"

"No, Rehan. His arteries show no major blockages," he replied.

"How do we explain it, then?" I asked, surprised.

"MSIMI," he said.

I stared blankly.

"Mental Stress-Induced Myocardial Ischemia," he explained.

"But he never seemed stressed…" I mused.

"That's the insidious nature of chronic stress. The body adapts outwardly, but internally, it triggers a destructive cascade. Chronic stress floods the body with cortisol and adrenaline. Over time, these hormones inflame blood vessels, destabilize plaque, and spasm coronary arteries. No blockage is needed," he continued.

"I spoke to his wife. He was consumed by work, had no hobbies, slept barely five hours, and freelanced at all hours."

Dr. Raj Kiran cited a Journal of the American College of Cardiology study: nearly 30% of heart attacks in professionals under 40 are stress-induced.

"That sounds like most doctors' routines. We're all at risk," I said, glancing at Dr. Raj Kiran, a workaholic himself. After his wife's death, he'd buried himself in work, which became his favorite pastime.

I understood his implication. There had been a recent surge in young patients with heart attacks despite lacking traditional risk factors like hypertension, smoking, or diabetes. Stress was the invisible culprit, and modern lifestyles would only exacerbate it.

What's the solution?" I pressed.

"We must organize our workloads and prioritize destressing through yoga, meditation, deep breathing, vacations, or hobbies. Anything that rejuvenates."

True. But the first step is acknowledging we're stressed. Most healthcare providers—doctors, nurses, technicians, executives—are high-risk groups for chronic stress, yet rarely admit it or act.

Dr. Prathap's ordeal was a wake-up call: no career milestone justified sacrificing health. Healthcare institutions must prioritize their workers' well-being as fiercely as patient care. As individuals, professionals must internalize that self-care is not selfish. It is survival.

During a meeting with Mr. Anand, I raised employees' mental health. He agreed it needed attention.

"As a hospital, we value our staff's health. We conduct annual checkups. What else can we do, Dr. Rehan?"

"The Perceived Stress Scale self-assessment has flaws. What if we mandate psychiatric evaluations and psychological counseling alongside checkups?"

"An excellent idea. It could help employees address undiagnosed anxiety, depression, or stress."

Thus, we implemented a policy integrating mental health assessments into our employee wellness program. The response was overwhelmingly positive.

On Dr. Prathap's discharge day, I advised him,

"Slow down. Prioritize yourself and your family."

"It took a heart attack to teach me that. I hope others learn before it's too late."

You're easily replaceable at work, but not to your family. Slow down before life forces you to.

*****

Two months after Dr. Prathap's heart attack, the institution's first-ever staff cricket match had materialized. It was not just as a game, but a rebellion against the unrelenting grind of medicine. The cricket field sprawled like an emerald oasis under the cerulean sky. The "Hope Ray Tigers," led by the boisterous CT surgeon Dr. Shekhar, faced off against my team, the "Hope Ray Eagles," in a 20-over showdown. The air hummed with laughter and the scent of freshly cut grass, a symphony of respite for souls accustomed to the cacophony of code blues and monitor alarms.

The teams were a mosaic of hierarchies and specialties forgotten. Dr. Raj Kiran, usually hunched over angiograms, stood tall as a slips fielder, his creased brow softened by the sunlight. Dr. Prathap, now on light duty, umpired with exaggerated gusto, his stent-free heart beating to the rhythm of camaraderie. Junior residents, often invisible in the hospital's pecking order, cheered wildly as consultants fumbled catches. Dr. Padmavati, Dr. Vimala and Shabnam were in stands cheering both the teams.

The Tigers batted first. Dr. Shekhar, wielding his bat like a scalpel, carved boundaries with surgical precision. His 80-run blitz, punctuated by sixes that sailed over the boundary ropes, was a masterclass in controlled aggression.

Chasing 181, the Eagles' innings began with Dr. Nithin and me at the crease. Nithin, our stoic orthopedic surgeon, transformed into a fearless slogger, his bat cracking like thunder. I, the "captain" by default, played cautiously—a reflex from years of weighing risks in the ICU. Together, we piled 130 runs, our partnership a silent pact to prove that joy could coexist with responsibility.

But cricket, like medicine, is merciless. Nithin holed out to midwicket, and I followed soon after, my stumps rattled by a yorker from Dr. Arun, the radiologist with a cannon arm. The collapse was swift. We crumbled under pressure and fell short by 10, but the scoreboard felt irrelevant.

The post-match feast was a carnival of dropped facades. Dr. Mohan Varma, the neurologist, queued meekly for biryani beside interns. Dr. Raj Kiran, still in his cricket whites, recounted a botched catch with self-deprecating humor. Even Dr. Shekhar, the victor, insisted the Eagles "let us win to keep morale high."

As I sat beside Shabnam on a checkered picnic blanket, she gestured at the scene. "Look at them. No phones, no charts—just people."

I nodded, watching Dr. Prathap teach his son to hold a bat. "For a few hours, the world didn't need saving. We did."

Shabnam peeled an orange, her voice tentative. "Do you think this… lightness… could last?"

I hesitated. That morning, I'd received three missed calls from the ICU. "Maybe not. But today proved we're more than our titles. A surgeon who drops a catch is still human. A healer who laughs is still healing."

She sighed. "We'll return to the chaos tomorrow."

"Yes. But now we know the antidote."

Months later, as monsoons lashed the city, Dr. Prathap gifted me a framed photo from the match. In it, Shabnam and I—mid-laugh, grass stains on our knees—embodied a truth medicine had buried: we heal best when we let ourselves be healed.

The inscription read: "To the Eagles' Captain—who reminded us that sometimes, the best way to save lives is to stop… and play.

CHAPTER 15

Give the ones you love wings to fly,
roots to come back and reasons to stay.

–Dalai Lama

It was the year 2017.

Sometimes, all you need is a break. As a doctor, you spend so much time with your patients or become so absorbed in their problems that you lose social connections with relatives and friends. When a friend calls or visits unexpectedly, it feels rejuvenating—a reminder of life beyond the clinic. So, when I received an unusual call from an old college mate, I was pleasantly surprised.

"Hi, Rehan! Guess who's calling," said the voice. It was unmistakable.

"Hey, Sheetal! How's everything?" I asked, startled.

Sheetal had been my college mate in medical school, intensely competitive, with whom I'd shared some tense moments.

"I'm good. Glad you recognized my voice. I thought your mind only registered special voices… like Shabnam's." A deliberate jab.

"Sheetal, you haven't changed!"

"And you, Rehan—have you?"

"No," I replied softly.

"Anyway, I called to let you know our batch is hosting a 25-year medical college reunion next month."

"Wonderful! Where?"

"Our first picnic spot: the hill station of Araku," she replied, laughing.

"A nostalgic choice."

"Don't miss it. I'll share the details with Shabnam too."

Indeed, it brought back memories of our first trip to Araku. Shekar, Naveen, and Kamal had planned the trip with meticulous care. Every detail, from the packed lunches to the winding route through the Eastern Ghats, was a testament to their zeal for adventure. But it was Shabnam who etched that journey into my memory forever.

On that trip, as the train plunged into the tunnel's darkness and then emerged, a slant of sunlight pierced the compartment, illuminating her like a staged scene. Gone was the shy colleague I'd known; in her place was Shabnam, transformed—her hair tousled by the breeze, kohl-rimmed eyes catching the light, a loose scarf draped over shoulders that seemed to carry newfound confidence. The moment felt suspended, as if the world had paused to unveil her reinvention.

Araku unfolded in a tapestry of emerald hills and coffee plantations, its air thick with the scent of earth and possibility. That evening, as we huddled around a crackling bonfire, Shabnam's laughter gave way to vulnerability. Her voice, softer than the rustling pines, wove stories of a fractured childhood, dreams deferred, and a hunger to rewrite her legacy. The firelight flickered across her face, each confession a thread binding us closer.

Years have passed since that trip, yet the memory lingers like the afterglow of sunset. We were just travelers then, chasing novelty. Little did we know Araku's forests held more than scenic vistas; they cradled the seeds of who we'd become.

This time, Sheetal threw herself into organizing the event, her zeal evident. She created a WhatsApp group with all the plans and updates related to our reunion. A week later, Ravi, my former roommate and closest friend, called. Now a pediatrician settled in the UK with his family, he said,

"You've heard about the reunion, right? Sheetal's leaving no stone unturned. I'm flying to India for this. Let's catch up properly!"

Missing it was unthinkable.

The reunion was a triumph. Sheetal's arrangements were flawless: the resort, exclusively ours, glowed under twinkling lights, nestled in Araku's serene, mist-kissed hills. Two decades had left uneven marks. The women seemed ageless, radiating vitality, while the men sported rounded middles and silver streaks. Yet, our camaraderie felt unchanged. Time collapsed into laughter and shared memories. Conversations revealed divergent life paths, but the warmth of reunion eclipsed differences.

The evening unfolded with spirited song-and-dance acts, a comic skit, and a glamorous fashion show. Shabnam dazzled, slipping into roles with ease. I, ever the observer, lingered at the edges, content to watch.

By the bonfire, I turned to Ravi. "Nostalgic, isn't it?"

"Absolutely. It feels like yesterday," he replied.

"Friends do that—make time irrelevant. You feel young again."

"What surprises me is how easily we all reconnect."

"That's the point of reunions—rediscovery," Sheetal chimed in, her voice bright.

"Sheetal, we've had years to set things right," Shabnam added, joining us.

"Shabnam! You, me, Rehan—the trio forever locked in rivalry," Sheetal teased.

"You misunderstood back then, just as you do now. It wasn't rivalry. It was passion for excellence," Shabnam countered gently.

"True. Maybe I was too envious to see it clearly, I see now you'd have cheered for either of us," Sheetal conceded.

"Exactly. What matters is giving your best," I said.

"Long ago," I added, "when I was adrift, Shabnam pushed me to compete. When I finally beat her, she wasn't bitter. Know what she said?"

"Good friends make each other excel," Shabnam finished, smiling.

"We could've been friends," Sheetal mused.

"We can be friends," Shabnam, Ravi, and I chorused.

"Hi, Rehan! It's been ages!" called Srikanth, joining our group. Our perpetually witty classmate had lost none of his humor.

"We've missed your jokes, Srikanth. You're truly one of a kind," I replied.

"Remember those Ouija board nights?" he laughed. "We scared the living daylights out of everyone! Though I always predicted you'd win that gold medal."

"You did? That's incredible!" Sheetal exclaimed, her eyes widening.

"No surprise there, Sheetal. Everyone knew Rehan was destined for it," he said with a wink. Shabnam and Sheetal exchanged a pointed glance.

"What about the 'master batsman'?" interjected Shekar, our former college cricket captain.

"Medicine bowled him out!" Ravi quipped. "But I hope the poet in him still survives."

"Survives? Who could forget Rehan's Ode to Shabnam?" Srikanth teased, grinning at her flushed cheeks.

"Rehan, you've been a wallflower all evening," Sheetal chided gently. "But we'll settle for nothing less than your latest poem."

"Before we leave, I'll share it—promise," I said, smiling.

Under a star-strewn sky, we traded stories, healed old rifts, and laughed until dawn's light crept in. It was the balm I hadn't realized I needed. Later, sleepless and inspired, I let the night's magic spill onto paper.

Life is beautiful!

In the bright gleam of the morning sun,

In the charm of the radiant full moon,

In the gentle touch of the falling dew,

In the cool embrace of the lovely breeze,

In the soft rustling of the tree leaves,

In the chatter of the noisy birds,

I found something beautiful.

In the lovely radiant smiles,

In the elegant sartorial choices,

In the heartfelt, meaningless laughter,

In the candid friendly banter,

In the soulful mellifluous voices,

In the zestful grooving dances,

I realized something beautiful.

In the camaraderie excellently shared,

In the bygone stories remembered again,

In the secrets that were finally broken,

I know that life is beautiful.

Life is but a collection of moments.

In our quest for happiness,

It's not the moments we add to life that matter,

But the life we kindle within each moment.

When we parted ways in Araku, I handed Sheetal the poem.

"You've captured it perfectly," she said, her voice soft.

"Only because you orchestrated the perfect night," I replied.

We carried Araku's magic home with us: the scent of rain-soaked hills, the echo of shared laughter in bamboo forests, and hearts lighter than they'd been in years. But the true treasure wasn't just the memories; it was the quiet certainty that Shabnam, with her sunlit stubbornness and storms-of-old wisdom, would walk beside me long after the trip faded into sepia-toned nostalgia. This time, she wasn't just a fleeting silhouette. She was the dawn breaking after a lifetime of twilight.

*****

When we returned to Hyderabad, I felt compelled to reconnect with our past. One weekend, Shabnam and I took our elder daughter Inara and son Ishan to Sunshine High School, where we had studied. Both children attended St. Joseph's School—a sprawling institution with modern amenities, a stark contrast to Sunshine's modest beginnings.

As we stepped out of the car, I gestured toward the weathered building. "This is where your mother and I started our journey," I said. "I wanted you to see our roots. Our humble beginnings."

Inara stared wide-eyed. "Oh… it's so small and old!"

When we entered the school premises, the watchman recognized us and escorted us to the office. Mrs. Jaya, our former science teacher and now headmistress, greeted us with delight. "It makes us proud to see how far you've come," she said, beaming.

"Madam, I'd like to give back to the school as a token of gratitude," I offered.

Her smile faded slightly. "The school is strapped for funds, Rehan. We're struggling."

"It'd be our duty, and pleasure, to help," I assured her, already forming a plan.

"Why not join our Republic Day celebrations?" she suggested. "The students would love to hear from you."

"I promise I'll be here," I said.

*****

It was January 26, Republic Day.

I stood on the same podium where I had once delivered morning prayers as school captain. This time, though, I was a guest speaker addressing the students.

"I am Dr. Rehan. My story begins in humble, middle-class roots—my father a banker, my mother a homemaker. As a student, I was careless, nonchalant, and far more enchanted by cricket bats than textbooks. But destiny, as it often does, had other plans.

Teachers like Mrs. Jay, Haema, Girija, and Vyjayanthi transformed me. Their unwavering belief, paired with a nurturing environment, turned an indifferent student into a school topper. Yet, I am not unique. Many of my friends seated here today share similar journeys—proof that strong roots allow you to branch out fearlessly and withstand life's fiercest storms.

We return to these roots today to express gratitude. And as I close, I borrow wisdom from Robert Frost:

'But I have promises to keep,

And miles to go before I sleep.'

I've honored some promises, but the road ahead remains long. My greatest hope? That each of you finds your purpose—a north star to guide you through your own miles, your own storms."

Later, in Mrs. Jaya's office, Shabnam and my former classmates—Arun, Ashok, Mohan, and Prakash—gathered with me. Through a WhatsApp group, our batch had avidly pooled donations for the school's renovation.

"Madam, this is a small token of our gratitude," I said, handing her two cheques. "The first is from me, earmarked for the Tenth Standard school topper. The second is a collective contribution from our batch for renovating senior classrooms, sports facilities, and the library."

Mrs. Jaya's eyes glistened as she smiled. "This isn't small. It is a significant sum!"

Shabnam nodded. "Madam, nothing we give could ever match what this school gave us."

That evening over dinner, we recounted the day's events to Inara and Ishan.

"You both went to a small school, yet you achieved so much. How did you manage that?" Inara asked.

"Size doesn't matter, Inara," I replied. "What matters is what happens inside. We had extraordinary teachers here who shaped young minds. A school's greatness lies in its teachers, your curiosity, and your drive to excel."

Shabnam added warmly, "And a few good friends to keep you motivated and grounded."

16

CHAPTER 16

*Don't be seduced into thinking that
that which does not make
a profit is without value.*

–Arthur Miller

It is said that all good things must eventually draw to a close.

My tenure as Medical Director had been a profoundly enriching chapter. It allowed me to heal not just through medicine, but through systemic change. While I remain, first and foremost, a physician at heart, the role gifted me a unique vantage point to impact patients' lives beyond the confines of clinical practice. I also completed a Master of Hospital Administration (MHA) program, equipping myself with the necessary credentials and comprehensive knowledge in healthcare management. It deepened my understanding of our patients' struggles, connected me intimately with every department, and forged bonds with our tireless staff. The CEO and hospital administrator championed my initiatives unreservedly, and together, we propelled Hope Ray toward higher standards of care.

Yet, subtle tremors had begun to ripple through the management's vision—shifts in priorities I failed to decipher, perhaps blinded by my immersion in patient care. The dissonance between their definition of "growth" and mine remained a quiet enigma. It persisted until the day it erupted, unannounced and unforgiving.

The reckoning arrived on an unremarkable Tuesday.

Mr. Anand Krishna, our administrator, whose laughter once buoyed boardroom tensions, stood rigid in my office doorway. The absence of his trademark grin felt like a shift in the weather.

"Dr. Rehan," he said, the words ash-dry, "I'm afraid our partnership… has reached its end."

A cold twinge of unease tightened my chest. This was unfathomable. Mr. Anand had enjoyed impeccable standing with the entire hospital; together, we had designed and executed transformative initiatives. What could have provoked such an abrupt severance?

I set down the patient chart I'd been annotating. "What's happened? Has the board raised concerns?"

"Transferred. To Vizag." He avoided my gaze, fixating instead on the NABH accreditation plaque we'd hung together. "Effective immediately."

"After everything we've built?" My voice tightened. "The mortality benchmarks? The residency program? The accreditation?"

"The board wants profit metrics now. Throughput quotas. Revenue per bed, not recovery rates." His knuckles blanched against the doorframe.

I knew administrators were judged by revenue generation, but I'd assumed our financial health was stable. Still, whispers had circulated lately about "aggressive measures" to compete with neighboring corporate hospitals.

"But we've proven quality care fuels sustainability—"

"To us, yes." His smile flickered, a dim echo of its former warmth. "To them? We're overhead waiting to be trimmed."

The handshake that followed carried the weight of a eulogy. Even as his footsteps faded down the corridor, I clung to a futile hope: that Mr. Anand might return, that principled work could still prevail. Long after he vanished, the ghost of his sandalwood cologne lingered—a requiem for the vision we'd interred

*****

The criteria for becoming an administrator are often unclear. When selecting doctors for roles, we evaluate a defined set of credentials: qualifications, professional experience, specialized skills, abilities, and overall demeanor. However, the process for choosing administrative staff can differ significantly. While merit and expertise remain factors, success in such positions often hinges on intangible elements, such as the ability to influence key decision-makers or proximity to those in power. These dynamics can propel individuals swiftly into leadership roles, even if traditional qualifications are lacking. The appointment of Mr. Nayak, our new administrator, exemplifies this reality

Mr. Nayak began his career as a front desk executive, where his responsibilities included patient registration and reception duties. Dissatisfied with the role, he transitioned to the marketing department, where he strategically cultivated connections with influential professionals. His career reached a pivotal moment when he facilitated Hope Rays successful recruitment of Dr. Karan Shetty—a distinguished neurosurgeon and star consultant at Gemini Hospital, a leading corporate healthcare institution. This breakthrough not only showcased his networking prowess but also propelled him into the upper echelons of management, cementing his reputation as a rising strategic leader.

How did this happen?

Mr. Kamal Ray, Managing Director of Hope Ray Hospital, was a detached leader who delegated medical operations to CEOs and administrators, preferring to focus on non-medical business ventures. His perspective shifted abruptly after a severe accident left him with a debilitating lumbar disc injury. Determined to receive the best care, he sought out top-tier neurosurgical expertise—a challenge, given that Hope Ray's neurosurgical team was inexperienced at the time.

He was advised to consult Dr. Karan Shetty, a renowned neurosurgeon at Gemini Hospital, a leading corporate healthcare rival. Despite initial reluctance, Dr. Shetty agreed to perform the surgery at Hope Ray under exceptional circumstances. The results were transformative: Mr. Ray's pain vanished, his mobility returned, and he became adamant about recruiting Dr. Shetty permanently. However, the surgeon repeatedly declined offers, wary of leaving his prestigious position.

Enter Mr. Nayak, Dr. Shetty's brother-in-law. After transitioning from receptionist to marketing executive, Nayak recognized an opportunity to elevate his career by leveraging his personal connection. He persuaded Dr. Shetty through a blend of familial appeal and a lucrative compensation package, culminating in a high-profile hospital transfer that stunned the industry.

This coup instantly established Nayak as the management's golden boy. When Hope Ray later faced intensifying competition from newer corporate hospitals, the leadership turned to Nayak for strategic solutions. It was a testament to his serendipitous rise. Sometimes, success hinges not on credentials, but on being in the right place at the right time.

*****

Seated at the head of the boardroom table, Mr. Nayak surveyed the department heads with a calculating gaze, his eyes dissecting their body language. Many were familiar faces from his earlier days at the hospital, though the staff's perception of him remained divided. To some, he embodied the aspirational underdog—a former frontline employee who'd clawed his way up, ethics notwithstanding. To others, his role demanded qualifications he lacked, making his ascent an affront to meritocracy.

"I mean business, nothing else," he began, slicing through the tension. "Every individual in this hospital must contribute, and every square foot must generate revenue. Perform or perish. That's the mandate."

A heavy silence descended; the air thick with unspoken tensions. The clinical setting now felt indistinguishable from a corporate war room.

"Before bringing me a problem," he added coldly, "ask yourself: Does it serve the hospital's bottom line? If not, solve it yourselves—or don't solve it at all."

As the meeting disbanded, I approached him, my unease outweighing caution. "You've made your stance clear. But isn't this approach… overly transactional?"

He turned, his smile devoid of warmth. "Dr. Rehan, we're not saviors—we're a business. Patients are consumers; healthcare is a service. Adapt or be replaced."

In that moment, I realized the true challenge ahead. The storm wouldn't rage from external competition, but from the erosion of purpose within.

Chapter 17

*We could never learn to be brave
and patient, if there were
only joy in the world.*

–Helen Keller

Seasons of change often herald the arrival of new individuals who can either introduce refreshing transformations or become skeptics, disrupting all that is good. Unfortunately, Mr. Nayak, the new administrator, embodied the latter. His presence loomed over the hospital like a storm cloud, his sharp features and perpetually furrowed brow signaling a man more accustomed to ledgers than laughter. Clad in stiff, charcoal-gray suits, he carried an air of austerity, his eyes darting behind wire-rimmed glasses as if already calculating the cost of every heartbeat in the building.

My first encounter with Mr. Nayak unfolded with unsettling precision. He entered my office without knocking—a trespass masked as confidence—and fixed me with a gaze so penetrating it felt surgical.

"Dr. Rehan," he began, his voice clipped, "we haven't formally met, but I'm acquainted with your… reputation. Likewise, I trust my own requires no introduction."

I rose, extending a hand I hoped concealed my unease. "Welcome, Mr. Nayak. I look forward to collaborating."

His handshake was brief, cold. "Collaboration implies alignment. It's important we must occupy the same page. Disagreement is a luxury this institution cannot afford."

"That depends on the page's contents," I replied, maintaining a calibrated tone. "We'll agree when priorities serve patients, staff, and this hospital's healing mission. All else warrants dialogue, doesn't it?"

"Ah." His lips curved into a smile that never touched his eyes. "You misunderstand, Dr. Rehan. My mandate is unambiguous: maximize revenue. Every decision I make will service that objective."

The air thickened. Somewhere down the hall, a monitor beeped a steady, urgent rhythm. "Then we'll align," I said carefully, "provided your decisions honor our oath to first, do no harm."

For a heartbeat, the room's temperature seemed to drop. "Harm is a relative term," he remarked, adjusting his cufflinks. "Financial anemia kills hospitals faster than ethical quibbles."

He left then, the door clicking shut with finality. I stared at the vacant space he'd occupied, my coffee gone cold. The encounter had lasted three minutes. It felt like a diagnosis.

Upon his arrival, Mr. Nayak's first decisive action was to install CCTV cameras in every corridor, nursing station, and even the break rooms. While this decision could have been framed as a measure to enhance security, his motivations quickly became clear. For him, the cameras were a weapon of control, not protection. He transformed his office into a surveillance hub, where he spent hours hunched over monitors, scrutinizing every gesture and interaction. Nurses were chastised for lingering too long at a patient's bedside; janitors were berated for pausing to sip water. "Efficiency," he declared in a staff memo, "is the antidote to complacency."

At the inaugural strategy meeting, Mr. Nayak unveiled a contentious proposal: all employees aged 55 years or older would be mandated to retire. I immediately raised my concerns.

"This decision is untenable. Nearly a third of our workforce falls into this category. Are we prepared to strip them of their livelihoods overnight?"

"Dr. Rehan," he retorted, "we're hemorrhaging funds on inflated salaries for senior staff. Replacing them with younger hires slashes payroll costs and boosts efficiency."

"You're reducing this to spreadsheets," I argued. "These individuals aren't liabilities. They're our institutional backbone. Their expertise, judgment, and loyalty are irreplaceable. Dismissing them won't just degrade care quality—it'll erode our moral foundation."

"Training can bridge the gap," he dismissed. "This directive comes from above. My role is execution, not debate."

A hospital thrives on equilibrium: seasoned veterans and driven newcomers. Senior staff anchor crises with decades of wisdom, guide complex cases, and mentor juniors. Younger teams inject innovation and vigor. Remove the veterans, and this symbiosis collapses. Patient outcomes, not profits, will bear the cost.

The proposal ignited fierce resistance across the room. Colleagues exchanged uneasy glances; some voiced objections outright. It was clear: the management's short-sighted pragmatism had underestimated the value of legacy—and the storm it would unleash.

"Very well," Mr. Nayak conceded, rising from his chair with a shrug. "If the seniors insist on clinging to their roles, there's a compromise: retain their positions at half their current salary. My hands are clean." He strode toward the exit, his tone final. "Take it or leave it."

The cruelty of the "compromise" hung heavy in the air. For veteran employees with mortgages, children's education fees, and aging parents to support, a 50% pay cut was a harsh sentence cloaked in false benevolence.

In the lobby, Mr. Nayak paused, turning to me with a chilly smile. "Dr. Rehan, loyalty to management isn't optional. You're expected to align with leadership priorities, not play advocate for dissenters."

"Advocating for our staff is advocating for the hospital," I countered, my voice steady. "Demoralizing experienced teams harms patient care. Alignment shouldn't mean blind compliance."

He chuckled, a sound devoid of warmth. "Idealism is a luxury this institution can't afford. Adapt to pragmatism, or you'll find yourself sidelined very soon."

"Thank you for the advice," I replied, pausing mid-stride. "But I'll stick to my principles. Pragmatism without empathy isn't strategy—it's erosion."

Our footsteps echoed through the sterile corridor. His retreating, mine resolved. The battle lines were drawn, not just over policy, but over the soul of the hospital itself.

That evening, I unraveled the day's frustrations to Shabnam over steaming cups of chai, the porcelain warm against my palms. Her fingers brushed mine, a fleeting touch as steady as her spirit, before I poured out the storm inside me.

"I feel utterly helpless, and it's infuriating," I confessed, the words sharp with exhaustion. "As Medical Directors, we're tasked with designing protocols for patient care and safety. Yet when we raise concerns about those very patients or our staff, we're stripped of authority. The title is just ceremonial, a hollow honor. We have no power to halt wrongdoing, no voice in executive decisions. Worse still, the administration dismisses our counsel as if it were noise."

Shabnam listened; her gaze fixed on the amber liquid swirling in her cup. When she finally spoke, her voice was a balm, soft yet unyielding. "Rehan," she began, "we can only mend the fractures within our reach. You've fought with every tool you possess—your voice, your logic, your heart. But some storms…" She paused, her sigh merging with the evening breeze. "…rage beyond any one person's control."

The weight of her wisdom settled between us, thick as the monsoon humidity.

"Stay true to your convictions," she continued, her hand resting on my forearm. "Not every battle is won in boardrooms. Sometimes, it's the quiet acts of integrity, the ones no policy can quantify, that outlast the clamor of greed."

Her reassurance coiled around me like a lifeline, simple yet unshakable. For the first time that day, the vise around my chest loosened. Beyond the window, stars pricked the twilight sky, their light defiant against the gloom. A resolve crystallized within me: I would appeal directly to the CEO. Not as a subordinate seeking permission, but as a physician bound by oath to shield both healers and those they heal.

"Thank you, Shabnam," I said, rising from my chair. "For the clarity… and the courage."

She smiled then, a fleeting, radiant arc of light. "Always."

18

CHAPTER 18

We cannot change our past.
We cannot change the fact that
people act in a certain way.
We cannot change the inevitable.
The only thing we can do is play
on the one string we have,
and that is our attitude.

–Charles R. Swindoll

Mr. Narender Acharya Rao, the revered CEO of Hope Ray Hospital, was a luminary whose name had become synonymous with transformative leadership. Celebrated not just for his visionary acumen but for the moral compass that guided every decision, he wielded integrity like a surgeon's scalpel—precise, unwavering, and untainted by compromise. His empathy, however, was his true hallmark. It radiated in the way he paused mid-stride to kneel beside a grieving family in the hallway, or how he remembered the names of every janitorial staff member, inquiring about their children's schooling with genuine interest. To work under him was to witness a masterclass in humanity fused with purpose.

He was a mentor who saw potential in raw ambition, he personally recruited me as a physician and, recognizing the impact of my work, later appointed me Medical Director—a role I embraced under his steadfast guidance. His mentorship was neither coddling nor distant; he challenged me to defend every proposal with data and heart. I'd present a plan for a free community clinic, and he'd dissect it in contemplative silence, fingers steepled, before asking, "How do we ensure dignity, not just diagnostics?" His approval was hard-won but transformative, as much a lesson in ethics as in execution.

Mr. Narender's open-mindedness was not passive acquiescence but an active pursuit of equilibrium. He hosted monthly "Voices of Hope" forums where nurses, technicians, and even patients' families could pitch ideas. I once watched him absorb a janitor's suggestion about ergonomic supply carts with the same intensity he'd later reserve for a million-dollar equipment proposal. "Innovation," he often said, "isn't confined to labs or budgets. It lives in the gaps where people dare to care. To him, the term innovation was indeed a covenant—a sacred vow to marry audacity with mercy. When the board resisted his push for a mental health wing, arguing it lacked profitability, he retorted, "Our ledger isn't just financial. It's measured in lives reclaimed."

As Medical Director, I spearheaded numerous transformative initiatives that garnered his enthusiastic endorsement. These included the establishment of specialized clinics for chronic diseases, securing prestigious NABH accreditation, launching a DNB residency program, and pioneering a state-of-the-art Critical Care Command Center. Each endeavor was designed to elevate patient care and institutional excellence. But none of this would've been possible without Mr. Anand, the administrative architect to my clinical vision. Together, we were alchemists, turning Mr. Narender's vision into gold. Our triad functioned like a precision instrument: Mr. Narender's moral compass, my clinical audacity, Anand's operational genius. Weekly strategy meetings dissolved into debates about ethics versus efficiency, but always ended with shared laughter and renewed purpose. We weren't just colleagues; we were custodians of a promise to prove that scale and compassion weren't mutually exclusive. When the board praised Hope Ray's 40% revenue surge, Mr. Narender Rao deflected credit: "This isn't growth—it's proof. Proof that doing right by patients is good business."

Mr. Anand's abrupt transfer struck with the violence of a summer storm. It was a tempest that uprooted the fragile ecosystem of trust we'd nurtured over decades. His absence wasn't merely a vacancy; it was an amputation. For years, he had been the unseen architect of Hope Ray's soul, the quiet maestro who harmonized my clinical fervor with the hospital's beating heart. Together, we were more than partners. We were counterweights, balancing audacity with pragmatism, passion with precision.

The news of Anand's transfer arrived via a sterile, three-line email: "Effective immediately." No farewell gathering, no clichéd plaque for his long years of service. Just a hollow echo where his laughter once ricocheted off boardroom walls. What tectonic shift had compelled Mr. Narender, the man who'd once postponed a shareholder meeting to personally console Anand during his wife's illness, to sever this alliance? This was the same CEO who'd dubbed us his "trinity of progress" at the annual gala, raising a toast to "the scalpel, the abacus, and the conscience." Rumors slithered through the corridors: whispers of boardroom coups, veiled threats from investors eyeing quarterly returns over patient outcomes. Had Mr.Narender's refusal to slash the palliative care budget been the spark? Or was this the first domino in a larger, darker design? The appointment of Mr. Nayak as Anand's successor only deepened the mystery.

Anand's transfer wasn't just a personnel change. It was an obituary for the Hope Ray we'd built. And I, the reluctant heir to its unraveling, stood at the precipice of a war not just for the hospital's future, but for its soul.

In the stillness of the sleepless night, I replayed Mr. Narender's cryptic words at our last meeting: "Even lighthouses must weather tides, Rehan."

A warning? A confession?

Determined to reclaim clarity, I resolved to confront him directly the next morning. There was something I was missing… I wanted to discover that missing piece. My eyes awaited the dawn to unravel the mystery.

*****

On that Saturday morning, I arrived at the CEO's office with a fragile thread of hope coiled in my chest. I paced outside his office, rehearsing arguments under my breath. The walls, lined with accolades and framed photos of him celebrating patient recoveries, offered only fleeting solace. After an interminable wait, his secretary finally gestured me inside.

Stepping into the office, I froze. The CEO sat behind his obsidian desk, but it was the figure in the leather guest chair that seized my attention—a stranger with a posture too polished, too predatory.

"Dr. Rehan," the CEO began, steepling fingers that trembled faintly, "you've arrived at a… pivotal moment." His voice, once a resonant baritone, frayed at the edges. He gestured to the man opposite him, who rose with the liquid grace of a knife being unsheathed. "Meet your new CEO. He assumes command next week."

The man turned.

Time folded. The tailored brown suit and silk tie dissolved, replaced by the memory of a school uniform stained with envy.

More than twenty-five years had passed since I last saw him. I vividly remembered that final day at school: he stood stunned by an unexpected defeat, his venom reserved for the one boy he'd always despised. As he stormed away, he spat, "This isn't over!"

Who could have imagined our paths would collide again decades later? Yet there he stood before me— my childhood nemesis, long forgotten but instantly recognizable, his smile sharpening into that same malevolent curve.

"Rehan!" He spread his arms in a parody of warmth. "The universe has a wicked sense of humor. Who'd have thought we'd meet like this?"

"Indeed, a cosmic jest… It's a cruelly small world," I replied, my voice steady despite the shock thrumming beneath my skin like live wire.

It was Sunil—once my tormentor, now the new CEO of Hope Ray Hospital.

19

CHAPTER 19

*Greed is a bottomless pit which
exhausts the person in an endless
effort to satisfy the need without
ever reaching satisfaction.*

–Erich Fromm

Life has a curious habit of circling us back to the same souls—not by accident, but to settle unfinished battles or spark revolutions within us.

Sunil had always been a creature of relentless ambition, his competitive streak carved into his bones since our school days. For years, he wore the crown of the class topper like armor, basking in the envy of peers and the pride of teachers. That is, until Shabnam and I emerged as contenders. Where Shabnam's brilliance was quiet and methodical, mine was fueled by stubborn grit, a contrast Sunil loathed. He sabotaged my projects, mocked my assignments, and even bribed the librarian to "lose" my reference books. Yet every trap he laid only hardened my resolve. By the time we reached 10th grade, the unthinkable happened: I clinched first rank. I'll never forget how he'd stared at the results pinned to the bulletin board, fists trembling, his face a mask of rage and humiliation. "Mistake," he'd hissed to no one in particular. "This has to be a mistake."

When we parted ways after graduation—Shabnam to medical school, me to a modest college, and Sunil to an elite private university—none of us could have imagined destiny would braid our paths together again, decades later, in the sterile halls of Hope Ray Hospital.

*****

Sunil's trajectory diverged sharply from ours. Medicine bored him; numbers were his religion. While Shabnam dissected cadavers and I memorized drug interactions, he devoured economics journals and case studies. His ascent was meteoric: a Harvard MBA secured not through charm, but by outmaneuvering 800 applicants in a simulation-based admission trial. Rumor had it he'd slept three hours a night for two years, surviving on black coffee and a vendetta against anyone who doubted him.

Returning to India, Sunil joined a fledgling pharma startup—a decision peers called "beneath his pedigree." Within five years, he'd transformed it into an industry titan. He slashed bloated budgets, forged ruthless alliances, and marketed a single diabetes drug so aggressively that competitors dubbed it "Sunil's Silver Bullet." By 35, he was the youngest Managing Director in the sector, a fact he celebrated by buying a vintage Rolex once owned by his childhood idol, Ratan Tata.

His reputation reached Kamal Ray, Hope Ray's besieged chairman, during the hospital's darkest hour. Plummeting stocks. A brain drain of senior doctors. Board members whispering about sell-offs. Desperate, Kamal attended a Mumbai conference where Sunil was keynote speaker. Colleagues later gossiped that Sunil had dismantled a skeptical investor's argument with such surgical precision that the man left the room mid-lecture, flushed crimson. Kamal approached him during the coffee break, mesmerized by the cold fire in Sunil's delivery. "You don't heal hospitals with band-aids," Sunil had said, swirling his espresso. "You burn them down and rebuild from the ashes."

The offer came the next morning: CEO of Hope Ray, with carte blanche to restructure. Industry veterans scoffed. "A businessman running a hospital?" they sneered. But Kamal knew Hope Ray needed a predator, not a physician. And so, with a signature sharp enough to slice paper, Sunil claimed his throne—unaware that the boy he'd once tried to destroy now worked two floors below him, saving lives in the ER.

*****

When Shabnam heard of Sunil's ascension to CEO at Hope Ray, her lips tightened into a frown.

"I don't have a good feeling about this," she mused, stirring her tea absently.

"You never know with Sunil," I replied. "If anything, you might be dealing with a meaner version of him now."

"It's double trouble with both Sunil and Nayak aligned," she countered, setting her cup down with a clink. "Their agendas will feed off each other."

I sighed, rubbing my temples. "It's going to get far more difficult for me, Shabnam."

"I know." Her voice softened. "They'll use your shoulders to fire their salvos—force you to execute their plans. And if you resist…"

"They won't hesitate to replace me," I finished flatly.

She leaned back, her gaze sharpening. "A real conundrum."

"What should I do?"

"Hold your ground. Fight for what's right, for as long as you can." Her tone hardened with conviction. "That's all that matters."

"Even if I lose?"

"Yes." She met my eyes, unflinching. "Some battles are worth fighting regardless of the outcome. Sometimes just showing up for your beliefs… that's the victory."

*****

The first meeting with the new CEO left the hospital's boardroom overflowing with physicians, their unease thickening the air like a gathering storm. Every chair was occupied; some doctors stood stiffly along the walls, arms crossed, eyes narrowed. All waited to see what vision this corporate prodigy would impose on Hope Ray.

Sunil strode to the podium, his tailored suit a stark contrast to the white coats in the crowd. He dispensed with formalities like a surgeon excising dead tissue.

"Let's skip introductions and address the battle ahead," he began, his voice crisp. "My mission is simple: redirect Hope Ray's trajectory from stagnation to dominance. Past achievements mean nothing if we lose the corporate race. And to win—" he paused, scanning the room, "—I require your unconditional cooperation. From today, performance will be measured by financial contribution. Numbers don't lie. Patient admissions, procedures, lab revenues—these are your KPIs. Mr. Nayak will outline the changes."

Nayak rose with a grin that didn't reach his eyes, unfolding a document like a prosecutor presenting evidence. The reforms were ruthless:

- 25% hike in diagnostic fees, room charges, and procedural costs.
- Pro bono cases strictly prohibited.
- No new staff recruitment.
- No new equipment proposals.
- Academic funding suspended; pharmaceutical sponsorships prioritized.
- Palliative Care Ward project terminated.
- Visiting consultants permitted to admit, treat, and operate—external partnerships incentivized.
- 20% service fee levied on all physician earnings.
- Revenue audits mandated for salaried consultants.

The stifling silence broke only once during the meeting, when Shabnam rose from her seat, her voice cutting through the boardroom's clinical air like a scalpel.

"And what of patient care, safety, or service quality?"

Sunil paused, fingertips drumming the polished table.

"Dr. Shabnam," he replied, his tone slick with faux deference, "we'll leave those… softer concerns to Dr. Rehan."

Murmurs rippled through the crowd. My jaw tightened. His dismissal hung like a toxin—reducing ethics to an afterthought, a burden to be pawned off.

The rest of the session revolved around profit margins, revenue streams, and financial calculus. Not a syllable spared for compassion. Not a clause addressing dignity.

As physicians filed out in grim silence, one truth hung heavier than the rest: the soul of Hope Ray had been sold.

CHAPTER 20

*The real man smiles in trouble,
gathers strength from distress,
and grows brave by reflection.*

–Thomas Paine

The new CEO, Sunil's reforms cleaved Hope Ray Hospital into two warring tribes. On one side stood the old guard—seasoned physicians like Dr. Raj Kiran, a silver-haired cardiologist whose stethoscope had outlived three CEOs; Dr. Mohan, brilliant neurologist whose gentle demeanor masked a spine of steel; Dr. Wilson, the fortuitous nephrologist with a penchant for quoting Hippocrates; and Shabnam, whose quiet brilliance anchored the Critical Care Unit. They were joined by a handful of idealistic physicians and residents, still bright-eyed enough to believe medicine was a calling, not a transaction.

Opposing them swelled a new breed of clinicians: sharp-elbowed proceduralists and entrepreneurial diagnosticians who viewed patients as revenue streams. They spoke the language of "throughput" and "monetization," their loyalty tethered to their payrolls. To them, a crowded OR schedule was a badge of honor, even if it meant cutting corners on appropriate protocols or dismissing a junior's concerns about a borderline angiogram.

The surge in revenue emboldened Sunil and Nayak, convincing them they were on the right path as they pressed forward with sweeping reforms.

Sunil's strategy bore grotesque fruit within a year. Patient admissions ballooned, the ER's triage board perpetually blinking FULL. Surgical suites ran 18 hours daily, their floors slick with the hurried footsteps of overworked nurses. The Cath lab became an assembly line, with stents deployed like clockwork, while the endoscopy wing resembled a factory, its scopes barely cooled between procedures.

The finance department reveled in the delirium. Revenue shattered projections, climbing 47% year-over-year. New doctor hires flooded the halls—strangers in white coats who nodded curtly in passing, their eyes glued to productivity dashboards on their phones.

But beneath the glittering metrics festered rot.

Simultaneously, a darker trend emerged. It was starkly visible in the hospital's monthly clinical governance meetings. Mortality rates crept upward. Post-procedural complications multiplied. Surgical site infections, once rare, now spiked alarmingly. Patient complaints flooded in: botched diagnoses, rushed discharges, consent forms signed under duress. Investigations revealed a pattern of reckless case selection, procedural shortcuts, and in some instances, gross negligence born of hurried arrogance.

Nayak shrugged off the data, his indifference as clinical as the spreadsheets he worshipped.

"As long as we meet targets, none of these matters," he snapped, waving away my report like a bothersome fly.

"These failures in patient care will haunt us," I countered. "We need to talk to the consultants and enforce the protocols!"

"You will not derail progress," he hissed, leaning across his desk. "The CEO called last quarter 'transformational.' We are not course-correcting."

"This isn't right—not ethically, not medically," I said through gritted teeth.

"Ethics?" He smirked, snapping his ledger shut. "The board approved a 28% profit margin. We've never been more right."

*****

During a routine postoperative consultation, I examined a CABG patient distressed by a swollen, erythematous sternal wound. Cultures from the purulent discharge revealed MRSA, a drug-resistant strain confirming a surgical site infection (SSI). After initiating targeted antibiotics, I logged the case and escalated it to the infection control team.

Nurse Meena, the infection control lead, called the following day. "It's baffling, Dr. Rehan," she said. "No comorbidities, optimal BMI, yet he developed an SSI. But there's more—he underwent an unplanned re-exploration immediately post-op."

"Documented reason?" I asked, already dreading the answer.

"Officially, 'postoperative hemorrhage.' But the drains showed minimal output, and his vitals were stable. It doesn't add up."

"I'll speak to Sandra," I replied, hanging up with a tightening chest.

The nursing director, Mrs. Sandra, met me in the dimly lit records room, her voice hushed. "The re-exploration wasn't for bleeding," Sandra confessed, her eyes darting to the door. "The surgeon left a retained swab. They only caught it on a postoperative chest X-ray."

"So, they lied in the notes," I muttered, fists clenching. "No hypotension, no bloody drains—just negligence."

She nodded grimly. "Nayak knows. He ordered us to bury it. The CT surgeons are revenue stars this quarter. He won't risk their 'morale.'"

"This is indefensible," I hissed. "A retained swab? MRSA? How many more incidents are we hiding?"

"You know the rule now," she said bitterly. "Generate revenue, and your sins vanish."

It was everywhere. Botched procedures swept under rugs. Near-misses buried in audit logs. Profit had become both sword and shield, excusing incompetence and eroding ethics.

As I left the room, the weight of complicity pressed like a lead apron. Hope Ray wasn't just failing patients. It was betraying them.

Later that afternoon, I found Dr. Raj Kiran in the cardiology wards dimly lit break room, his weathered hands cradling a chipped mug of tea. Desperation sharpened my voice as I recounted the swab incident, Nayak's indifference, the metastasizing rot in our protocols.

He listened in silence, the lines around his eyes deepening. "I've watched three CEOs gut this hospital's soul," he said finally, setting down his mug with a clatter. "Sunil's different—he doesn't just want profit. He wants domination."

"How do we fight this?"

"We outlast it." His gaze hardened, the steel of a man who'd survived a hundred boardroom wars. "Storms pass, Rehan. Even the worst of them."

His calm was infuriating. I left him with fragile hope.

That evening, I found Shabnam pacing the terrace, her silhouette framed against the amber glow of the city. The weight of Gemini's offer pressed against my ribs like a second sternum. For weeks, Hope Ray's moral decay had gnawed at me—the cover-ups, the commodification of care, Sunil's smirk etching itself into every compromised decision. Now, this lifeline.

Gemini Healthcare had been established long before Hope Ray and was revered for the pioneering work of its founder, Dr. Krishnamurthy, widely regarded as the father of corporate hospitals in India. What began as a small clinic in Hyderabad had expanded nationwide with multiple branches. Gemini was known for delivering high-quality healthcare services and had since diversified into pharmacy chains, diagnostics, health insurance, and home care. Hope Ray had always aspired to match its stature.

"Gemini Hospital reached out today," I began, my voice steadier than I felt. She turned, her eyes narrowing at the name.

"They want me to jump ship. Take others with me."

Shabnam froze. "Gemini? The Krishnamurthy legacy?"

"What do you think, Shabnam? Should we take that leap of faith?" I asked.

"Rehan, you need to think about this carefully," she said skeptically. "You don't know what's in store for you at Gemini."

I was torn…

And then COVID happened!

Chapter 21

The greatest enemy of knowledge is not ignorance; it is the illusion of knowledge.

–Stephen Hawking

In 2020, COVID-19 made its way to India, altering life as we knew it.

COVID-19 was an adversary unlike any we had ever faced. When I diagnosed our first case, I couldn't fathom the tsunami that would follow. The hospital plunged into chaos. Government health officials swarmed our corridors. Over 80 staff members, myself included, were quarantined. Headlines splashed Hope Ray's name in panic-stricken ink. Sunil, usually a maestro of strategy, stood paralyzed—a CEO outmaneuvered by a virus.

A coalition of consultants, primarily surgeons and salaried physicians, approached Sunil with growing unease. "Patients are avoiding Hope Ray, terrified of contracting COVID-19," they argued. "Declare us a non-COVID hospital. Restore public trust, and revenue will follow."

Nayak, ever the pragmatist, endorsed the proposal with zeal.

At the emergency committee meeting, Sunil's gaze swept the room before settling on me. "Rehan, our physicians demand we prioritize non-COVID cases. They claim this will stabilize our patient inflow and finances. Your thoughts?"

"A catastrophic idea," I countered. "This pandemic will explode. If we close our doors now, we'll drown when the wave hits."

Nayak scoffed. "Fear mongering! Cases are negligible. We're bleeding revenue today. Must we bankrupt ourselves for hypotheticals?"

"Hypotheticals?" I snapped. I stabbed a finger toward the window, where a harried nurse sprinted across the parking lot, her PPE suit crinkling in the midday sun. "That 'hypothetical' is coding a patient in the ER right now! You think they're staging drills for fun?"

"Enough." Sunil's fist struck the table, silencing the room. "Hope Ray is hereby a non-COVID facility. We reconvene in two months to reassess."

I stormed out, the acid tang of betrayal sharp on my tongue. In the corridor, a junior resident hesitated, her mask slipping as she clutched a stack of unused ventilator requisitions. "Dr. Rehan, the isolation ward...?"

"Cancel the orders," I muttered, not meeting her eyes.

Later, in the parking lot, I sat gripping my steering wheel as rain lashed the windshield. Sunil's Mercedes glided past, its headlights cutting through the gloom. You'll see, I thought, watching his silhouette shrink in the rearview mirror. By the time you realize your mistake, we will drown in the COVID tsunami.

*****

The following two months unfolded like a nightmare scripted by a malevolent force. COVID-19 cases erupted exponentially, metastasizing from isolated clusters into an uncontainable deluge. The virus seeped into every corner of the city: tenements, high-rises, even the guarded enclaves of the elite. Government-mandated lockdowns came in frantic waves, each announcement more desperate than the last. But the measures proved futile against the pathogen's ruthless arithmetic.

Public hospitals buckled first. Corridors became makeshift wards, echoing with the cacophony of coughing fits and the shrill alarms of crashing oxygen monitors. Bodies wrapped in plastic piled up in parking lots, awaiting cremation slots. Overwhelmed interns triaged patients on the fly, their faces etched with exhaustion beneath fogged goggles. Meanwhile, Gemini Hospital, poised with its vast resources, absorbed the lion's share of critical cases, its glossy ad campaigns now replaced by grim tallies of "ICU beds available."

Hope Ray, however, languished in eerie silence. Its spotless wards stood vacant, monitors blinking idly, as if frozen in time. The "non-COVID" strategy, once touted as a masterstroke, collapsed spectacularly. Nayak's spreadsheets, once flush with projections, now hemorrhaged red ink. The hospital's reputation cratered; headlines mocked its abandonment of civic duty, while families of former patients protested at its gates, clutching photos of loved ones denied treatment.

For the staff, the impotence was excruciating. Surgeons renowned for pioneering cardiac procedures now twirled pens in empty clinics. Nurses, trained in advanced critical care, sterilized unused equipment. I'd find Shabnam staring at the vacant ICU, her gloved hands clenched. "We're healers," she'd mutter, "reduced to spectators."

Revenue plunged, but the moral bankruptcy cut deeper. Board members fretted over quarterly dividends, while clinicians drowned in quiet shame. The virus, it seemed, had exposed a rot no policy could mask: Hope Ray had traded its Hippocratic soul for the illusion of safety, only to find itself stranded on the wrong side of history.

22

CHAPTER 22

Between stimulus and response,
there is a space. In that space is
our power to choose our response.
In our response lies our
growth and our freedom.

–Viktor Frankl

Frustration is a peculiar emotion. It coils around your psyche like a venomous serpent, its fangs dripping with doubt and inertia. When Hope Ray Hospital abruptly suspended COVID-19 admissions, that serpent tightened its grip on me. The corridors of the hospital, once buzzing with the urgency of saving lives, fell silent. My days, once defined by the rhythm of rounds, and consultations, dissolved into an abyss of helplessness. Medicine wasn't just my profession; it was my identity. To stand idle during a pandemic, when every instinct screamed "Act!", felt like a betrayal of my oath. The administrative decision, though framed as a "strategic pause," struck me as a surrender to fear. My hands, trained to heal, now hung uselessly at my sides. Depression crept in, not as a dramatic collapse, but as a slow suffocation—a relentless whisper that I had failed my purpose.

It was during this vulnerable chasm that Gemini Hospital's executives found me. Their call came on a Thursday afternoon, while I sat in my home office staring at a blank computer screen, willing myself to draft a research paper I no longer had the heart to complete. Mr. Ranjan, Gemini's HR Vice President, spoke with a disarming calmness. "Dr. Rehan, we'd like to discuss a matter of mutual interest," he said, as though proposing a casual lunch. His tone carried neither the brashness of a corporate recruiter nor the desperation of a rival institution. It was measured, almost empathetic. When I hesitated, he added, "Ten minutes. That's all I ask."

The Taj Hotel's lobby was a study in contrasts to Hope Ray's sterile halls. Marble floors gleamed under crystal chandeliers, and the air smelled of jasmine and freshly brewed coffee. Mr. Ranjan stood near a grand piano, his balding head catching the light as he waved me over. Beside him stood Mr. Amar, Gemini's senior marketing head, whose sharp suit and sharper gaze hinted at ambition. They resembled chess players—poised, calculating, yet unfailingly polite.

"Thank you for coming, Doctor," Mr. Ranjan began, clasping his hands. "Let me be candid. We've followed your work for years. It's remarkable. But we also know Hope Ray's current policies have... restricted your capabilities." He paused, letting the implication hang. "Gemini wants to change that."

His offer was staggering: double my salary, full autonomy over my department, and the freedom to bring my entire team. For a moment, the numbers blurred. This wasn't just a job. It was an endorsement of my value, a lifeline thrown when I'd begun drowning. Yet, beneath the allure, unease stirred. Hope Ray wasn't just an employer; it was where I'd spent 20 years building a legacy. The residency nights spent napping in on-call rooms, the tears shared with families of terminal patients, the pride of mentoring young interns—these weren't memories I could auction to the highest bidder.

"Your loyalty does you credit," Mr. Amar interjected, as if reading my mind. "But loyalty shouldn't chain you to stagnation. Imagine what you could achieve with Gemini's resources." He slid a brochure across the table: state-of-the-art ICUs, robotic surgical suites, a research wing rivaling Europe's best. The subtext was clear: You're wasting your potential.

That evening, I recounted the meeting to Shabnam, over chai in our dimly lit garden. A psychiatrist with a knack for dissecting motives, she listened quietly before responding.

"Gemini's timing is strategic," she observed, stirring her tea. "They're capitalizing on your frustration. But hospitals like theirs thrive on branding, not altruism. What happens if their priorities clash with yours?" Her skepticism mirrored my own doubts. Gemini, though prestigious, had a reputation for aggressive expansion and whispers of prioritizing profitable elective procedures over critical care during the pandemic.

"Remember Dr. Mehra?" she added. Our friend had joined a corporate chain in 2019, lured by promises of autonomy, only to quit a year later, alienated by bureaucracy. "It's not just about money. It's about whose vision you'll serve."

Her words crystallized my conflict. At Hope Ray, I'd fought to keep patient care at the center, even when budgets tightened. But Gemini's offer dangled something irresistible: influence. With their platform, I could scale my outreach, pilot public health initiatives, perhaps even reshape their ethics from within. Was that naïve idealism?

The next morning, I wandered Hope Ray's deserted COVID wing. Sunlight streamed through windows onto empty beds, their mattresses stripped bare. A faded "Thank You, Doctors!" poster, signed by recovered patients, fluttered on a wall. I recalled Amma, the 70-year-old grandmother who'd squeezed my hand after surviving a month on the ventilator. "You're my angel," she'd said. Now, her bed was a hollow frame.

Dr. Raj Kiran, my mentor, once told me, "Hospitals are living organisms. They thrive on the souls of those who serve them." Hope Ray's soul felt fractured now, its heartbeat muted by boardroom decisions. Yet, walking past the pediatric ward—still bustling with laughter despite the crisis—I wondered: Could I abandon the place that raised me?

Weeks passed. Gemini's offer lingered, a shadow over every decision. I dissected their contract, scrutinizing clauses about "performance targets" and "brand alignment." I met former Gemini staff at discreet coffee shops, probing for unvarnished truths. Their accounts were mixed: praise for cutting-edge tools, frustration with profit-driven quotas.

One conversation stood out. "You'll have power," said a retired Gemini surgeon, "but you'll fight for it daily. Corporate medicine is a different beast."

Ultimately, the choice hinged on a single question: What kind of healer do I want to be? At Hope Ray, I was a known entity—a leader clinging to eroding ground. At Gemini, I'd be a catalyst, albeit one navigating minefields.

The answer came during a midnight downpour. Shabnam found me pacing the study, Gemini's contract strewn atop my old medical journals. "You're afraid," she said softly. "Not of failure, but of regret."

In that moment, clarity struck. My value wasn't tied to an institution, but to the lives I touched. Whether at Hope Ray or Gemini, I could uphold my oath if I retained the courage to fight for it.

"At least at Gemini, I'd actually practice medicine" I said, staring at darkened windows. "Here, I'm just a bystander to collapse."

Shabnam studied me, her silence more potent than words. Finally, she murmured, "You've always followed your conscience, Rehan. Do it now."

"I met their vice president of HR yesterday," I admitted, the words tasting bitter. "The offer's unchanged. I… I think I'm going to accept."

She didn't flinch. "Then meet their CEO. Settle terms."

"Tomorrow," I said, the commitment solidifying like cement in my chest. "We finalize the agreement tomorrow."

Her quiet nod felt like absolution.

*****

The phone rang at 11:47 p.m.

Nayak's voice slithered through the receiver, sharp with uncharacteristic urgency: "Emergency meeting. 8 a.m. CEO's office. Don't be late."

The emergency meeting convened at dawn in the CEO's cavernous office, its glass walls still streaked with rain from the night's storm. Sunil sat hunched at the head of the conference table, his tailored suit rumpled, eyes bloodshot—a far cry from the arrogant strategist who'd once dictated terms with a snap of his fingers. Spreadsheets littered the table, their red-inked losses screaming failure.

"Our strategy," he began, voice frayed, "has collapsed. While Gemini and public hospitals battled the surge, we've become irrelevant. Two months wasted. Two months our rivals used to cement their reputations." His gaze, heavy with unspoken blame, locked onto Nayak before shifting to me. "What now, Rehan?"

I leaned forward, the weight of wasted lives sharpening my words. "We return to our roots—patient care. Open every ward, every ICU bed. Prioritize triage, transparency, and treatment. No more hiding behind 'non-COVID' labels while people die at our gates."

Nayak scoffed, adjusting his gold cufflinks. "Sentimental nonsense! Our infrastructure isn't equipped for—"

"Your counsel," Sunil interrupted, slamming a palm on the table, "has cost us millions and our credibility. Sit. Listen. Learn."

The silence that followed was electric. Nayak's face flushed crimson, but he sank back into his chair.

"Your proposal, Rehan," Sunil demanded.

"We form a dedicated COVID task force: physicians, pulmonologists, critical care specialists, the Nursing Director, and medical social workers. They'll design protocols for triage, oxygen rationing, and family communications. Every decision," I stressed, "will be data-driven, ethical, and patient-first"

Sunil's nod was slow, almost reverent. "You'll lead this team. Full autonomy—protocols, staffing, resource allocation. Nayak," he added icily, "will handle logistics. Paperwork. Nothing more."

Nayak's pen snapped between his fingers. "This is—"

"Non-negotiable," Sunil finished, rising to his full height. "We're done here."

As the room emptied, Sunil lingered, his voice uncharacteristically quiet. "Don't make me regret this, Rehan."

"I won't," I said, though the weight of his gamble—and the lives depending on it—settled like stone in my chest.

$$23$$

Chapter 23

*Success is not measured by what
you accomplish, but by the
opposition you have encountered,
and the courage with which you
have maintained the struggle
against overwhelming odds.*

–Orison Swett Marden

The COVID-19 scourge raged relentlessly for over two years, its tendrils tightening around the city in waves of despair. Like every major hospital, Hope Ray became a battleground. Its corridors echoing with the rasp of ventilators, its walls steeped in the acrid scent of bleach and despair. Shabnam, Mrs. Sandra, and I spent countless nights hunched over blueprints in the dimly lit administration office, drafting protocols that balanced cold science with fragile humanity. We mapped screening strategies to separate the infected from the vulnerable, established red-green zones to prevent cross-contamination, and designed isolation wards with audio visual central monitoring. Oxygen tanks were rationed with military precision using algorithms. Death, when it came, was met with protocols for dignified body bags and grief counselors trained to deliver news.

Yet the true crisis lay not in logistics, but in the souls of those fighting on the frontlines. Shabnam transformed the ICU into a fortress of resilience, her voice steady even as patients coded beneath her hands. Nurses like Anika, a 23-year-old rookie, worked triple shifts in suffocating PPE, their faces bruised by N95 straps, their hands raw from sanitizer. Doctors collapsed in call rooms, only to jolt awake for the next emergency intubation. We became adept at mourning in stolen moments—a shared silence over burnt coffee.

Paradoxically, Hope Ray thrived financially. Our COVID wards operated at 100% capacity, insurance reimbursements flowing in as steadily as the ambulances. The board rejoiced at quarterly profits, oblivious to the moral cost.

If the first wave was a storm, Delta was a tsunami. The variant tore through the city with viperous efficiency, bypassing vaccines and youth alike. Mortality rates doubled, then tripled. Morgues overflowed; pyres burned through the night at crematoriums.

Everybody lost someone dear to them. I lost one of my young cousins. Our housemaid had a narrow escape. We saved many lives but we lost a few. Every life received the same frantic urgency—the same trembling hands adjusting oxygen flow, the same prayers muttered over IV lines. Grief became our universal language, spoken in the hollow eyes of colleagues and the muffled sobs echoing through isolation wards.

The ICU became a theater of impossible choices. One bed free: a 68-year-old grandmother or a 32-year-old father of twins? We wept. We prayed.

*****

Amidst the chaos, a single patient learned the true meaning of empathy—of care that was both selfless and unwaveringly efficient. And who could have imagined that patient would be Sunil?

One night, my phone rang urgently. It was Sunil.

"Rehan, I'm not well. I think I have COVID. I'm breathless… I'm coming to the ER."

I found him in the ER, brought in by his driver. He was febrile, his breathing labored, with a history of sudden-onset fever, cough, and breathlessness over the past 24 hours. His SpO2 hovered at 84% on room air; the COVID screening test was positive. The HRCT scan confirmed severe bilateral pneumonia.

"Rehan, save me," he gasped, his voice trembling with a desperation I'd never heard before. "I don't want to die."

We transferred him to the ICU and initiated high-flow oxygen, antiviral therapy, steroids, and supportive care. Shabnam met us at the doors, her calm presence steadying the chaos.

Sunil's eyes darted across the unit—18 patients, each on escalating oxygen support, several on mechanical ventilation. The relentless beep of monitors filled the air.

"Don't panic, Sunil," Shabnam said softly, adjusting his nasal cannula. "You'll improve."

"You really believe that?" he whispered, his CEO bravado crumbling. "Will I… see my family again?"

"You will," I said firmly, meeting both their gazes. "I promise."

In the next few days, Sunil's oxygen requirements increased, necessitating HFNC support. He lay in the COVID ICU, battling every day for his life. We arranged a tablet so he could talk to his wife and kids, but he often grew emotional—feeling helpless, scared, and alone. Shabnam and I visited him daily, keeping his spirits up and urging him to fight. On days when someone succumbed to COVID, he would break down.

One afternoon, as a code blue alarm echoed down the hall, he turned to Shabnam, his voice raw.

"You know what's worse than death, Shabnam?"

She waited, her silence a balm.

"Dying alone," he whispered, tears glinting in his eyes. "The terror of taking your last breath in a sterile room, surrounded by machines instead of loved ones…"

"Who said you're dying?" I interjected, squeezing his shoulder. "You're not alone. You've got two old friends here—Shabnam and me. Not everyone gets that privilege."

A fragile smile flickered across his face. "All my power, all my wealth… none of it shields me from this." He gestured weakly at the ventilator hissing nearby. "What a wretched epiphany."

He'd reflect on how arrogant and proud he had been in life, and how an invisible virus had brought him to his knees. He marveled at how we, his apparent opponents, had become his unexpected lifelines.

It took two weeks for Sunil to stabilize and begin a gradual recovery.

A day before his discharge, he held my hand and said, "Rehan, I was consumed by rage, pride, and arrogance. I couldn't see beyond my own shadow," Sunil admitted, his voice fraying with regret.

"You traded patient care for profit margins," I replied, the words sharp but steady.

"I treated people like spreadsheet entries—ignoring your warnings about staffing, equipment, infrastructure…" His sentence dissolved into a choked sob.

"And now? Do you finally see?" I pressed, softer now. "These doctors, nurses—they're giving pieces of themselves to save strangers. No hesitation. No second thoughts."

"I slashed budgets, stripped the ICU bare… All for numbers on a screen," he muttered, staring at his trembling hands. "But there are lines you can't cross. Some things… they're sacred."

"They're the pulse of this place," I said. "The heart, the soul—things no spreadsheet will ever quantify."

Sunil nodded slowly, tears glinting. "This… this is what I'll carry. Every damn day."

On his discharge day, Sunil gripped my hand, his palm clammy but firm.

"Thank you. For staying."

"We're healers," I replied, Shabnam's presence steady beside me. "This is what we do."

"I know you nearly left for Gemini," he said, catching me off guard. "Yet you stayed. Despite everything I'd done."

"Hope Ray needed us," Shabnam answered for me, her tone gentle but unyielding.

"You two…" He shook his head, marveling. "In school, I saw rivalry. Now? A partnership that moves mountains."

*****

Months later, Shabnam stood on a dais, the governor's "COVID Warrior Excellence Award" glinting in her hands. Cameras flashed as she lifted the trophy.

"This," she said, gaze sweeping over our team—nurses with scarred cheeks from PPE, interns who'd aged a decade in two years, "belongs to them. The ones who held hands when families couldn't, who whispered comfort into dying ears."

CHAPTER 24

Every storm runs out of rain.

–Maya Angelou

The world emerged from Covid's shadow like a patient taking their first unsteady breath after extubation—fragile, yet defiantly alive. At Hope Ray Hospital, the corridors hummed with a renewed rhythm. Machines beeped in steady cadence, masks still dotted faces like familiar scars, but the air crackled with an energy that transcended survival.

Mr. Nayak's transfer had been swift, almost surgical. In his place, Mr. Anand returned to the administrative helm, his presence a balm to staff still nursing wounds from Nayak's cutthroat policies. The change was palpable. Nurses lingered longer at bedsides, residents debated treatments without fear of reprisal, and the once-ubiquitous whiteboards tracking "revenue milestones" now displayed patient satisfaction scores in looping cursive.

On a serene Saturday afternoon, I was summoned to the CEO's office alongside Mr. Anand. Sunil greeted us with a faint, contemplative smile, his posture loosened by the weight of unspoken reflections.

He began, his voice steady yet tinged with revelation:

"For years, I believed medicine operated like any other business—a transactional exchange devoid of emotion. It was purely give-and-take, nothing more. But lying alone in that ICU bed, oxygen hissing through a mask while others around me gasped their final breaths... I realized medicine transcends profit. Rehan and Shabnam didn't just treat illnesses; they eased pain, quelled distress, and quieted fear. Not once did they prioritize anything but humanity. They didn't merely cure diseases; they transformed lives. That is something no corporation can replicate. Now I see clearly: I don't belong here. I'm resigning as CEO. This institution deserves a leader who grasps medicine's true essence. I've recommended you, Rehan, to the board as my successor."

For a moment, I stood silent, the weight of his words pressing against the stillness of the room. When I finally spoke, my voice carried the quiet resolve of a man who had long ago chosen his path:

"Sunil, I entered medicine to serve people. It is my passion—one I will pursue until my last breath. Hope Ray gave me more than a career; it offered a platform to transcend the role of a mere physician. But I've learned that aligning visions with those of differing ideologies is no simple feat." I paused, meeting his gaze. "Still, I'm grateful you now recognize what truly matters: empathetic care. For all of us here, the patient always comes first. That's why I must decline your offer. My next chapter awaits."

I extended my hand, the gesture bridging years of unspoken tensions. "Thank you. I wish you nothing but the best."

This time, our parting held no bitterness—only the quiet understanding of two men who had, at last, glimpsed each other's truth.

*****

Sunil stepped down from his position as CEO, making Mr. Anand the natural choice to succeed him. Hope Ray, a hospital that had lost its way, began finding its direction again. Mr. Anand abolished all the previous contentious proposals, placing a prime focus on patient care. The motto became delivering good quality care with reasonable profits. Mr. Kamal Ray, the Managing Director, appreciated the hospital for its sincere and dedicated work during the COVID-19 times. He realized that profits could still be made without compromising the quality of patient care. Consequently, he granted funding for Geriatric and Palliative Care wards, which were previously considered non-performing areas. He remarked, "Everyone can make money, but not everyone can win hearts."

Six months later, I met Mr. Anand in his office. He leaned against his desk, his eyes narrowing slightly as he assessed me. "Rehan," he began, a note of cautious optimism in his voice, "everything's progressing smoothly—clinical outcomes, quality metrics, even revenue. We're launching a new branch in Gachibowli. I'd value your and Shabnam's expertise in structuring the departments."

"That's remarkable news," I replied. "Shabnam will gladly contribute. As for me… I won't be available."

His pen froze mid-air. "What do you mean?"

"It's time I step back. I've given 25 years to Hope Ray. Now I need to forge my own path."

"You're not defecting to Gemini?" he asked, half-joking, half-apprehensive.

"Never." I met his gaze steadily. "This next chapter is mine to write. I'll share details when I'm ready."

"But how can you just leave?" he protested. "We've done so much together, and we could do so much more!"

"Mr. Anand, working at Hope Ray has been a profound experience. The hospital gave me opportunities, and I gave my best in return. We weathered turbulent times, and I stayed on to steady the ship. Your comeback gives me hope you'll continue prioritizing patients. As for me, I've decided to look beyond the present and carve out something rooted in my beliefs."

"But you can still do that here," he urged. "You'll have my full support."

"We both know that even together, we can't sustain change indefinitely. The corporate mindset will always shift. What you champion today, your successors might abandon tomorrow. I need to forge a new path—my path, a patients' path—one that remains unshakable, with strong roots."

"I understand, Rehan. But why leave me in the lurch now, when I'm just settling in?"

"I'm not abandoning you. I'm leaving Shabnam here until you've consolidated your position and strengthened this foundation."

*****

That evening, Shabnam turned to me and asked,

"Are you sure you're on the right path?"

"That's the only thing I'm sure about, Shabnam."

"What if you fail?"

"What if I succeed?"

For a moment, the weight of twenty years hung between us—the midnight emergencies, the lives salvaged, the quiet losses. Then her smile broke through, warm and rueful. "That's what I've always loved about you. Your courage to walk with conviction, no matter the outcome."

"And I couldn't do it without you by my side," I replied honestly.

"Then why ask me to stay behind?"

"Because I won't build something new by tearing down Hope Ray. Stay and support Anand through this transition."

"He doesn't grasp the scale of what's coming," she murmured, thoughtful.

"He'll be hurt. But in time, he'll adjust his sails."

Leaving Hope Ray wasn't easy. Two decades of memories had woven it into a second home; the staff, a family. Letting go felt like losing a part of myself.

Yet I walked away—without a goodbye.

25

CHAPTER 25

*Our deepest fear is not that we
are inadequate. Our deepest fear
is that we are powerful beyond measure.
It is our light not our darkness that
most frightens us. We ask ourselves,
who am I to be brilliant, gorgeous,
talented and fabulous? Actually,
who are you not to be?*

–Marianne Williamson

In the months following my departure, Hope Ray witnessed a quiet hemorrhage of its brightest minds. Dr. Raj Kiran, the visionary chief cardiologist; Dr. Wilson, the pioneering nephrologist whose protocols had redefined kidney care; and Dr. Mohan, the neurologist whose research had once put the institution on the global map, all vanished without fanfare. Their exits, like mine, came without press releases or farewell dinners, leaving only unanswered emails and empty clinics.

The pattern soon repeated across rival institutions. At Gemini Hospitals, oncology's rising star, Dr. Aisha Khan, closed her practice overnight. Sunrise Medical Center lost its entire elite gastroenterology team to cryptic early retirements. It was as though the soul of medicine had begun to fade. While specialists occasionally shifted between hospitals, the simultaneous exodus of diverse experts across multiple institutions was unprecedented—a seismic shift that sent ripples through the healthcare world.

The media dubbed it "The Silent Exodus." Editorial boards speculated wildly: corporate greed? Burnout? A clandestine collective bargaining effort? But the truth proved more disquieting. For the first time in modern healthcare, it wasn't institutions competing for talent. It was talent abandoning institutions. The corridors of power hummed with panic. Administrators scrambled to reverse protocols that prioritized profits over patients. Investors demanded answers. And in waiting rooms nationwide, people whispered the same uneasy question: If even the healers have lost faith, where does that leave the rest of us?

Meanwhile, my own mission demanded relentless focus.

The clock was ticking, and the weight of what I aimed to build pressed heavily on my shoulders. A year earlier, I'd begun laying the groundwork. My first meeting was with Dr. Raj Kiran, Hope Ray's charismatic chief cardiologist. Over chai in his cluttered office, I sketched my vision—a system where medicine prioritized patients, not profits. To my relief, he leaned back, steepled his fingers, and said, "Rehan, this isn't just bold. It's necessary."

Dr. Mohan and Dr. Wilson followed. The former, a neurologist with a reputation for diagnosing the undiagnosable, listened in silence before remarking, "You're asking us to gamble our careers." But by dawn, he'd drafted a list of conditions to safeguard ethical practice. Dr. Wilson, ever the pragmatist, grilled me for hours on sustainability before finally nodding. "Let's rewrite the rules," he said.

Shabnam remained Hope Ray's unwavering pillar long after my departure. Her expertise anchored departments through turbulent transitions, and Mr. Anand leaned heavily on her to spearhead quality reforms.

The real challenge? Scaling the vision.

Recruiting talent from corporate hospitals felt like defusing bombs. One misstep, and whispers of my plans would spread. Dr. Raj Kiran and Dr. Mohan were great help with their doctor contacts. I relied on old allies: residents I'd mentored, administrators disillusioned by bureaucracy, even a retired CFO with a grudge against shareholder-driven policies. Each conversation was a dance—probing values, testing loyalties, and ultimately, revealing just enough to ignite curiosity.

Then came the pharmaceutical puzzle.

I conducted a deep dive into the drug supply chain. The drug supply chain begins with manufacturers who produce medications and sell them to pharmaceutical companies. These companies then distribute the drugs to wholesalers or stockists, who supply retailers or pharmacists. Finally, the medication reaches patients through doctors' prescriptions. At each stage, margins inflate the cost—from manufacturing to MRP (Maximum Retail Price). By bypassing intermediaries and supplying directly to patients, the price could be drastically reduced.

One day, I called Muskaan.

"It's time we had a serious conversation," I said.

"Bored with Shabnam?" she asked, giggling.

"Shut up, Muskaan! I need you to set up a meeting with Azeem," I replied, explaining my plan.

During a tense dinner with Azeem and four other pharma leaders, I outlined our model: no kickbacks, no manipulated trials, only transparent partnerships.

"Our visions must align. I understand the supply chain dynamics and propose collaborating to deliver drugs directly from companies to hospital at half the wholesaler's price. Patients will pay the same purchase cost, far below MRP."

The group exchanged glances, deliberated briefly, and reconvened.

To my surprise, Azeem laughed. "You're either naïve or revolutionary. Either way, Star Pharma is in—and so are our top four. It won't be easy. We'll face fierce resistance, but we'll overcome it."

"Wonderful! Welcome aboard," I said, shaking hands with everyone.

My next challenge was diagnostics.

Integrating cost-effective diagnostic systems into hospitals posed a major hurdle, requiring careful balancing of operational costs, equipment expenses, reagent consumables, staff expertise, and quality accreditations. Prices fluctuated wildly depending on these variables. While many low-cost diagnostic centers dotted the market, luring patients with cheap rates, their reports were often unreliable. Yet I believed a quality-driven, affordable model was still achievable.

The person who could help me build this—and join the cause—was Dr. Vikas Mehta, founder of Lumia Diagnostics. Years earlier, he'd guided me through Shabnam's postpartum seizures when others faced a diagnostic dilemma. Now, I appealed to that same unwavering integrity.

"Do you know how these low-cost diagnostics actually work?" Vikas asked pointedly.

"Yes. Multiple factors determine the pricing," I replied.

"Costs drop when you use cheaper equipment, subpar reagents, untrained staff, and skip accreditations like NABL, ISO, or CAP. But that ruins report quality," he countered.

"What's the solution?" I asked.

"Invest in reliable equipment and quality reagents. Secure bulk purchase discounts and offset margins through high volume. Maintain accreditations at all costs."

"So, low-cost diagnostics with accuracy are possible?"

"Of course," Vikas said firmly. "If profit isn't your sole god."

"Dr. Vikas," I pressed, "your machines diagnose, but your protocols decide their impact. Join us. Let's ensure they serve patients, not profit quotas."

He signed on before the night ended.

Finally, the unsung heroes.

Mrs. Sandra, the Hope rays nursing director joined my bandwagon. We assembled a dream team: nurses who charted vitals with a healer's intuition, technicians who treated machines as extensions of empathy, and executives who measured success in recovered smiles, not spreadsheets.

Only Shabnam remained.

Every instinct screamed to bring her aboard immediately, but Hope Ray needed her steady hand. She'd hold the fort, guiding Anand and masking the void we had left, until the day our fledgling institution could rise without collateral damage.

*****

One Week Before Launch

Shabnam cornered me in the half-built lobby, her laughter echoing off unfinished walls. "This is madness, Rehan. A hospital run by idealists? They'll call you a fool."

"Or a visionary," I countered. "Raj Kiran was right. When profit isn't the pulse, medicine thrives."

Her gaze softened. "How did you even fund this... experiment?"

"The primary investments come from our core consultants, alongside contributions from other major investors. Remember MLA Manjunath? Saving his son didn't just shift his politics. It unlocked his goodwill and his coffers. He now holds a pivotal role in the Health Ministry and arranged a meeting with the Health Minister, where

I presented my proposal. Impressed by the model, the Minister affirmed the government's support for initiatives advancing public health and connected me with three international healthcare foundations eager to partner with us. Combined with the consultants' investments…" I gestured toward the skeletal ICU rising behind us. "This isn't just a hospital—it's a manifesto. Decisions are made by consensus, guided by a board of core consultants with patient care as the only priority. No CEO, no managing director. Just a shared vision."

"And its name?"

"MedLife Hospitals." Steel frames hummed around us like a promise.

"Where medicine doesn't just treat—it transforms."

Chapter 26

*We are all faced with a series of
great opportunities brilliantly
disguised as impossible situations.*

–Chuck Swindoll

MedLife seized the city's imagination from its inception. Whispers of its founding team—a constellation of the metropolis' most revered physicians and surgeons, each investing not just capital but their hard-earned reputations—ignited fervent speculation. This was no ordinary institution: conceived as a sanctuary for all, its manifesto promised elite medical care at grassroots affordability, delivered with an unwavering human touch.

The corporate world met MedLife with derision and disbelief. Industry titans dismissed it as a hollow publicity gambit; conspiracy theorists spun tales of shadowy agendas; pragmatists predicted its collapse within a fiscal year. "High-quality care at rock-bottom prices?" sneered a prominent hospital CFO in an interview. "A fairy tale for bleeding hearts."

Yet MedLife defied obscurity through the sheer gravitational pull of its founders—the city's most celebrated medical luminaries, now aligned under one banner. Skeptics scrambled to decode their motive. What unified these icons? editorials probed. Profit? Prestige? The enigma itself became fuel, igniting scrutiny from boardrooms, newsrooms, and grassroots advocacy groups alike.

MedLife chose July 1ˢᵗ—India's National Doctors' Day— for its historic launch, a date imbued with profound symbolism. The day honors the birth anniversary of Dr. Bidhan Chandra Roy, the revered physician-statesman and former Chief Minister of West Bengal, whose groundbreaking work reshaped public health infrastructure and inspired generations of healers. A man who famously declared, "The patient is the center of the medical universe," Roy's legacy of equitable care made the date a fitting crucible for MedLife's mission.

As the hospital's doors opened, the choice felt less like coincidence and more like destiny—a tribute to the timeless principles of compassion over commerce, humanity over hierarchy.

A few hours before the launch, Shabnam found me reviewing final protocols in the empty pharmacy. Her eyes widened as she gestured to the bustling lobby below.

"This feels unnervingly prophetic, like witnessing Atlas Shrugged unfold in scrubs and lab coats. A modern John Galt strike, but instead of industrial titans, it's a sanctuary forged by the world's sharpest medical minds and unshakable ethics."

"If only reality bowed to fiction's simplicity," I replied, my grin tinged with exhaustion. "MedLife as Atlantis—a pinnacle of pure medical idealism? A beautiful vision. But the world seldom yields to our grandest designs."

"And yet," she replied, her voice an awed whisper, luminous with pride, "you made it yield."

"Do you know the hardest part?" I asked, leaning against a shelf of yet-unstocked generics.

"Recruiting the doctors?"

"Precisely. Corporate hospitals aren't devoid of talent. They're full of brilliant physicians shackled by bureaucracy. They cling to ethics where they can, but survival binds them to compromise." I tapped a vial of insulin, its price tag slashed to a fraction of market rates. "I didn't recruit them. I offered them an alternative."

Shabnam's voice rang out, sharp and resonant. "MedLife!"

*****

At noon, the atrium swelled with surgeons in tailored suits, nurses in freshly pressed uniforms, and patients already clutching hope like talismans. I stepped onto the podium, the weight of stethoscopes and expectations heavy on my neck.

"Doctors, Diagnostics, and Drugs," I began, "are the pillars of any healthcare system. Yet, each comes with its own price tag. Today, patients face a labyrinth of choices— uncertain whom to trust or if their decisions are sound.

Consider physicians: some offer consultations at modest fees, while others command premium rates. Does a higher cost guarantee superior expertise?

Then there are medications. Brand-name originators, high-cost generics, and affordable generics flood the market. Prices fluctuate wildly, but does this reflect differences in efficacy?

Diagnostic services further muddy the waters. Identical tests vary in cost across facilities. Are pricier reports more accurate?

These dilemmas plague patients' minds, rooted in a tension between profit and compassion. What defines 'enough' in healthcare? How do we balance financial viability with empathy?

The answer lies in redefining value. Can we deliver excellence—top-tier doctors, precise diagnostics, and reliable drugs—at accessible prices? Absolutely. It begins with embracing sufficiency over excess, prioritizing care over greed.

Yes! By championing equity, we prove that quality and affordability can coexist. This isn't just possible—it's imperative."

The screen behind me lit up—a live dashboard comparing prices:

- Doctor consultations: Top doctors' consultations 50% below corporate rates
- Drugs: Top generics at 40% discount, sourced directly from ethical manufacturers
- Diagnostics: NABL-certified tests, 30% cheaper

Murmurs rippled through the room. A journalist's phone dinged—MedLife's website, already crashing under traffic.

"There's no CEO here," I continued. "No shareholders demanding quarterly growth. MedLife is governed by its physicians. Dr. Raj Kiran—" I nodded to the silver-haired cardiologist, "—will oversee medical strategy. And leading daily operations… Dr. Shabnam."

Gasps. Cameras pivoted to her. She stiffened, then stood, chin lifted—a queen accepting a reluctant crown. I watched Dr. Raj Kiran nod in solemn acknowledgment. Shabnam's startled expression betrayed her surprise—I'd kept this decision hidden from her and everyone else.

Later, over bitter hospital coffee, Dr. Raj Kiran approached me, his voice low but urgent. "Rehan, we bear a responsibility not to fail. The world watches us."

"Who could be better suited to guide us than you, sir?" I replied.

He stirred his coffee absently. "Years ago, when Hope Ray's then-CEO demanded I name a Medical Director, I answered 'Rehan' without hesitation. Do you know why?"

I remained silent, the hum of the cafeteria fading around us.

"Because you saw beyond personal ambition to the collective good," he said, fixing me with a piercing gaze. "Which makes your choice to pass the role to Shabnam… unexpected."

"MedLife has no hierarchy," I countered, pressing a hand to my chest. "We govern collectively. As Medical Director, I feared my biases might blind me. This way, we hold each other accountable."

I watched Shabnam across the hall, calmly dismantling a reporter's cynicism.

"Shabnam won't just lead. She'll inspire."

*****

Midnight found us on the rooftop, the city's smog momentarily hushed.

Shabnam and me under a sky ablaze with stars, the full moon casting its silvery glow over the city's distant hum. I had kept Shabnam in the dark about her impending role at MedLife, a decision that now hung in the air like the crisp night breeze. When I'd announced her name earlier that day—declaring she would helm the daily operations—her widened eyes and parted lips betrayed her shock. Yet I'd known she wouldn't hesitate to accept the responsibility. Shabnam was never one to shrink from a challenge, even when blindsided by fate.

"Why did you do that, Rehan?" she asked, her voice as soft as the breeze.

I turned to her, the moonlight etching resolve into my features. "Because you're my moral compass, Shabnam. When I falter, you steer me true. But with you in the lead, I don't have to worry. I know you will always do the right thing."

A smile bloomed on her lips, tentative yet luminous. "And what becomes of Rehan now?"

"Now," I said, my eyes reflecting the constellations above, "I return to where I've always belonged."

"Ah." Her laughter rippled through the darkness, warm and rich as spiced chai. "Being Dr. Rehan, MD—the physician who forgets to eat unless reminded." She shook her head, strands of hair catching moonlight like filaments of onyx. "Always chasing miracles with a stethoscope and a stubborn heart."

The city's heartbeat thrummed beneath us as her mirth faded into something quieter, softer—a vow sealed not with words, but with the weight of shared history. Above us, the stars burned brighter, as if the universe itself leaned in to listen.

We lingered, the future stretching before us—a fragile, audacious experiment.

Somewhere, a defibrillator charged.

Beeped.

Cleared.

A heartbeat restored.

MedLife's first night.

And for me, it was not the end.

I had a long journey ahead.

And miles to go before I sleep…